CW00547965

HER HUSBAND'S SECRETS

A COZY MYSTERY SET IN SPAIN

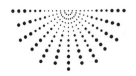

KATJA KLEIBER

Copyright 2023 by Katja Kleiber

c/o easy-shop

Kathrin Mothes

Schlossstrasse 20

06869 Coswig (Anhalt)

www.katja-kleiber.de

Coverdesign: bookbrush

This novel was first published in German in 2022 under the title „Riskantes Erbe - ein

Spanienkrimi".

Translation: DeepL

Editing: PJ Skinner

All rights reserved.

This work, including its parts, is protected by copyright. Any exploitation is prohibited without the consent of the author. This applies in particular to electronic or other reproduction, translation, distribution and making available to the public.

❀ Created with Vellum

CHAPTER ONE

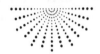

UWE COULD ALREADY SEE his babe in front of him. He had met the cute chick a fortnight ago during his last visit to the St. Georg district.

He would arrive soon. He had only seventy-five kilometres to drive to Hamburg, which was only a stone's throw away compared to the distance he had covered since he left Spain.

He glanced at the display, which showed the time in green digits. The countdown of the tachograph to the next rest break was running relentlessly. If he didn't get to his babe fast enough, he would have to drive to a rest stop and sleep in the truck. These modern tachographs were impossible to trick. Nor was his boss.

Fortunately, the motorway was empty at this time. The road was dry. He stepped on the gas to go a little faster than allowed; only a few kilometres per hour, still within the permitted limit. Slowly, the four-cylinder truck accelerated.

His headlights drilled tunnels of light into the darkness. A country song played on the radio and Uwe turned up the volume. He drummed along to the rhythm with his right thumb on the steering wheel. The music kept him awake, along with the amphetamine tablet he had taken. He took the pill shortly after Karlsruhe. Usually, he kept them in the glove compartment, but he found it reassuring to know he could rely on them. Now he didn't want to stop and rest because he longed for this cute little one with the mouse eyes but he couldn't fall in love. His job didn't allow it.

A glimmer of light illuminated the right-hand side of the road.

He squinted to see better.

Fire. Not a forest fire, he was too far north for that. An accident. A car had struck the right-hand crash barrier and caught fire.

Uwe applied his foot to the brake. At the same time, he pressed the button on the hands-free system and spoke "one, one, two" into the microphone. A calm voice from the emergency call centre answered and asked him for facts. While the articulated lorry slowed down, Uwe reported the accident.

Finally the truck came to a halt. He looked back up the still empty motorway. He jumped out of the cabin and ran across the empty lane.

The fire had engulfed the car. Flames shot up metres high. The outlines of the car body were only recognisable as a black skeleton.

Heat hit him in the face. Flakes of ash swirled through the air and landed on his shirt.

Uwe stopped. There was nothing left to be saved.

He stared at the wreckage. When the fuel tank went up, he didn't want to be near it.

He turned around and hurried back to his truck.

That's when he saw her.

A woman ran into the field that stretched beside the motorway. Away from the burning car. Her bright hair shone in the glow of the flames. Then the darkness swallowed her up. The wail of sirens approached from the distance. As Uwe reached the cab of his truck, an explosion tore the night apart.

CHAPTER TWO

IRENE LOLLED IN COMFORT; her eyes still closed. She felt for the warm body next to her to cuddle some more. Only the cold sheet met her fingers. She opened her eyes. She was lying alone in bed.

With difficulty she tried to remember why. Hubert had called on Thursday when he left Spain. He had promised to be with her bright and early on Saturday. But he had not arrived.

Irene closed her eyes again and turned onto her left side relieving the pressure on her right shoulder, which ached again.

Hubert had probably slept on the sofa so as not to disturb her. As he always claimed. In truth ... in truth, what? She didn't want to think about it. She massaged her shoulder. The skin felt dry. She needed to rub some body oil on it again. It had been a long time since her skin could manage without care.

She was too lazy to go into the living room and greet him. It wouldn't bother him if she dozed a while longer. It had been a long time since Hubert had woken her in the morning with caresses. She pulled the blanket up to her nose.

She heard a scratching sound in the hallway. A key turned in the lock. Had Hubert finally arrived?

"You're still in bed," trumpeted Jasmin. "Good morning, late riser!"

Irene wondered how could a night owl like her have a morning person for a daughter. She rolled out of bed and went into the bathroom. In the mirror she saw a wrinkled face and tousled shoulder-length brown hair. White roots were showing at the crown of her head; she would soon have to go to the hairdresser again. At fifty-one, she needed a few tricks to look reasonably respectable. The smell of coffee made her hurry the morning ritual.

When she came out of the shower, a glance into the living room confirmed that the sofa was empty. Had Hubert at least called to say he would be late? She looked at the phone. No flashing light on the answering machine. No message on the mobile either.

Irene shuffled into the kitchen.

She did not find Hubert there either, but her daughter set the table. Bread rolls and croissants were piled up in the bread basket. Jasmin stood at the cooker, carefully putting eggs into a saucepan.

"Hey, Mum." She turned and threw her arms around her neck.

As always, Irene marvelled at how quickly her baby had become a grown woman. In the summer she would have to buy thirty candles for her birthday cake.

A grey-striped cat mewed on the balcony. She put food in a bowl, opened the door and put it down for the cat. The cat had been watching her carefully. It mewed briefly and pounced on the food.

Irene watched as the animal devoured the chunks. The stray had appeared one day, jumping over the garage roof onto her balcony. Shaggy, with dull fur. The next time she went shopping, cat food had ended up in her basket. She turned away and went into the living room.

"Since when do you like cats?" asked Jasmin.

When she was little, she had always wanted a pet but it would have been too much trouble for Irene. She had assumed that the work of looking after it would fall on her. There was so much going on at their hotel that she sank into bed exhausted in the evening. After all, the mortgage she had bought the hotel with had to be paid off. What had seemed like a bargain turned out to be dilapidated. Cats had been the least of her worries.

Irene shrugged her shoulders, still too grumpy to answer.

"Where's Pop?"

Irene shrugged her shoulders. She couldn't answer that question. Too often Hubert had announced he would be home, then turned up much later or called to say his project had been delayed and he needed a few more days. But he had always been reliable. The day before yesterday, he had clearly said that he would be here on Saturday night.

The egg timer rang. Jasmin took three eggs out of the pot, rinsed them under cold water and placed them in colourfully painted ceramic cups. They were from her time as an intern in the five-star hotel on Mallorca, Irene remembered. That was ages ago, too. She forced her memory to be more precise. She had lugged the colourful egg cups around for more than thirty years, from the tiny home under the roof in her first shared flat with Hubert in Sankt Pauli to the long-awaited old building in Harvestehude.

A smell of waffles percolated through the kitchen. Jasmin piled the hot pastries on a plate and put a small bottle of maple syrup with them. Then she placed three red paper napkins on the plates and sat down at the table.

"Let's get started."

She did not say that there was no point in waiting for Hubert.

Irene took her usual seat overlooking the balcony and reached for the bread knife.

The telephone rang. Why didn't Hubert call the mobile? Irene rose.

"Good morning, am I speaking to Mrs Hansen?"

"Yes, Hansen speaking. I'll tell you right now, I don't order anything over the phone. Save yourself the trouble!"

Irene intended to hang up, but the serious tone of voice stopped her.

"Hamburg Criminal Investigation Unit, my name is Mo Davidoglu. I'm afraid I have to give you some sad news."

CHAPTER THREE

IRENE CLUNG to Jasmin's hand. It was just as cold as her own.

Jasmin wore sunglasses, even though the sky was overcast. You couldn't see her eyes but Irene knew they were red and swollen.

Her friend Suzie held her up on the other side. Her shock of bright red hair stood out against her black mourning clothes.

The pastor wore the enormous white collar of the Nordic Protestant Church.

His words passed her by. For days, a thin veil had hung between her and the world. The only thing she wanted was sleep and dream of times when her little world had still been intact.

"Ashes to ashes, dust to dust."

Someone thrust a shovel into her hand. What did they expect? Was she now to shovel cold earth onto this urn? An urn that contained Hubert? A jar full of cold ashes had replace his warm, living body. Her hand moved as if by itself, without her doing anything. With a dull sound, clods of earth hit the urn.

The red rose slipped from her fingers. She sobbed and turned away. Her daughter gently took the shovel from her. Irene staggered over to one of the tall trees that lined the row of graves. At least the ancient giants would understand her suffering with their centuries of experience. The smell of damp earth and lawn clippings intruded on her grief.

Suzie had followed her, and they embraced. They paused for a while. Irene sobbed until her throat went dry. Then she felt silly putting on such a show at the funeral. After all, Hubert's accident had been three weeks ago, she should have controlled herself. The prosecutor had ordered a post-mortem, which had delayed the funeral. The remains had been cremated afterwards, thank goodness. She couldn't have borne to see the dissected corpse. Or even the sight of a coffin with the dead body. The idea of a cleansing flame comforted her a little at least. She wiped her eyes and straightened up.

Suzie held out a chocolate bar to her. As if food would fix everything. She pushed her hand away and re-joined the others. Her relatives lined up to offer their condolences. Mechanically, she shook hands. An aunt, a cousin she hadn't seen in ages. Colleagues of her husband. She hardly heard the embarrassed words of sympathy.

At the same time, she remained somehow angry with Hubert. All the plans they had still had. Travel, new hobbies. For retirement. And now he had left, out of her life forever. She heaved a sob.

A woman approached her, took her hand.

She looked up.

The woman had very fair hair, individual strands were dyed light blue and pink. She was young, about the age of Jasmin, Irene estimated. A piercing disfigured one eyebrow, another her lower lip.

The woman leaned forward, whispered in her ear, "You lost him too." Still holding her hand tightly.

Irene took an involuntarily step back. At that moment Suzie intervened. She took the young woman by the shoulders and pushed her aside. The woman let go of Irene's hand. Suzie resolutely turned the woman around and led her away, down the path that led back to the chapel.

Irene watched them go.

Then Manfred van Vreeden approached her. She had last seen her husband's partner at an exhibition the architects had organised in their office. Promoting young artists or something. That was a year ago, she reflected. She felt happy then.

The slender white-haired man took her hand. "What a terrible misfortune. Hubert died far too young. My deepest condolences."

He spun around, holding her hand so that she had to follow his movement. Was she mistaken, or did he want to distract her from the encounter with the confused young woman?

"Please come and see us in the next few days so that we can settle some questions about Hubert's current projects," Manfred asked.

She nodded absently.

"As soon as you feel up to it, of course." He seemed to have realised what he was putting her through.

She wanted nothing more than to curl up on the sofa and sleep if possible. In her dreams, Hubert was always with her.

"You know he managed that hotel construction in Spain. I'm taking over now, but some things are unclear to me."

"I'm not familiar with his work."

"Still, we'll try."

"He hasn't talked much about what he does in the office," she objected.

"We'll see about that then. You, as his heiress, have to sign some papers anyway so that it can go on."

"I'll be happy to." She heard herself agreeing, although nothing was further from her mind than signing any powers of attorney for architects. What she actually longed for was peace and quiet.

An infinite calm, like the one Hubert enjoyed now.

CHAPTER FOUR

THE DISPLAYS RADIATED COLOUR. Oranges, persimmons, tomatoes, lush green cucumbers. Irene did not see the beauty.

She had dragged herself to the Turkish place on the corner. She was sure she wouldn't make it to the supermarket.

Day and night were still a blur. She dozed off in bed. She had no appetite either. Today she had dragged herself to the bathroom and seen her sunken face in the mirror. As a result, she had forced herself to go shopping.

Mechanically, she put some oranges in her basket, tomatoes and lettuce. The little shop on the corner didn't have a selection like the discounter, but it had the essentials, plus all sorts of exotic things like okra, stuffed vine leaves and other delicacies. She reached for food that she could eat cold. Irene didn't feel like cooking; she couldn't even get up the energy to do baking, her hobby.

She had left the running of the hotel to Jasmin for days. She could manage, at least for a few days or weeks. In any case, better than Irene could manage by herself in this state.

Irene felt better when she had filled her basket and was standing at the checkout.

The Turkish trader rounded down the sum, letting her off a few cents.

"Thank you," she murmured.

As she left the shop, she heard a bright voice behind her, "Hello."

She turned around.

A young woman, pierced and tattooed, her light hair coiffed into a tangled bird's nest.

Irene had seen the woman before, but where? She greeted her with a nod of her head and continued walking.

"Just don't imagine you'll inherit everything he owned."

The deranged woman from the cemetery! The one who had clasped her hand and talked nonsense.

Irene walked faster.

The young woman kept pace effortlessly. "I loved him!"

Irene put her bag down and turned to the pushy woman. She took a deep breath. "Leave me alone!" Unintentionally, her voice broke.

"Don't pretend you don't know anything!"

Irene snorted. "You have me confused with someone else. We don't know each other."

"I was Hubert's true love!"

Irene winced when she heard her husband's name.

"And the flat in Spain, I'll say it now, it's mine. After all, I have the keys!" At these words, the woman pointed to her own chest with her thumb. "You won't get them."

She turned abruptly and left.

Irene needed a moment to collect herself. Then she picked up her bag and lugged the shopping home. As she put the groceries in the fridge, the woman's words echoed inside her. Hubert's true love. Irene's thoughts were racing. The business trips to Spain to supervise the hotel project. All the overtime. Was there something she hadn't noticed?

She reached for her mobile phone, dialling Suzie's number as she left the kitchen to snuggle into a blanket on the sofa. Suzie's voicemail answered: "You have reached the Sunshine Yoga Studio. If I don't get back to you personally, I'm teaching right now. Please leave a message and I'll call you back."

Irene released a sob. Quickly she pressed 'hang up'. Hopefully quickly enough so that Suzie wouldn't notice her desperation. Otherwise she would be sure to come and cook for her, and force food on her she could barely choke down.

As soon as she hung up, her friend called back. "Just been to the toilet, how are you? How can I help you?"

"Oh, Suzie!" Irene incoherently described what had happened. That a crazed woman was stalking her. The same person who had approached her at the funeral.

Suzie listened to her for a while. Then Irene heard her take a deep breath.

"You really knew nothing?"

CHAPTER FIVE

THE NOTARY SAT ENTHRONED behind a mighty wooden desk. He had either bought it in an antique shop or inherited it. Probably the latter, when she looked at the office. Except for one colourful oil painting, an abstract work, the furnishings looked dignified but unobtrusive. Presumably, many generations of Hanseatic lawyers had amassed money to enable Doctor Wigbert Schwekendonk to run an adequate business.

Irene remembered the Formica table in the small kitchen where she had done her homework while her mother prepared dinner. Then she pushed the image away and concentrated on the notary's words.

He read out the will that Hubert had deposited with him, in a worn tone of voice. It mentioned current accounts, share funds, a life insurance policy. All things which could not bring her husband back.

Her thoughts drifted. Suzie had tried to make her understand as gently as possible that Hubert had indeed had a mistress - and probably for years. It was indeed the pierced one who had turned up at the funeral.

"She's no older than Jasmin," Irene had interjected, startled.

She had seen the two of them together in a restaurant, Suzie had said. Canoodling. And a few months later at an art opening.

"Why didn't you tell me?" What were girlfriends for anyway? Suzie wasn't usually reticent.

"I thought you knew," Suzie had replied lamely. "Would tolerate it."

Under no circumstances would Irene have tolerated a rival. She would have kicked Hubert out of the house.

Would she have? Or would she have remained silent, feigning ignorance?

The notary's voice came through to her, interrupting her thoughts. His tone had changed somehow.

"Of everything, your daughter inherits the compulsory portion, i.e. one quarter. However, your husband, who has now passed away, has left one of his assets to you alone; the Spanish company 'Daurada Ltda'. It will become your property in its entirety."

Irene looked at him uncomprehendingly.

"Making an inheritance in Spain requires some bureaucratic effort, as we know from other clients. We will of course be happy to assist you with that." The notary looked at her hopefully. "We also have relation-ships with local partners who are trustworthy."

Irene was stunned. "What kind of company?" The image of a factory appeared in her mind's eye.

The notary looked at the documents again. "No statement is made here about the nature of the business. The assets refer to a property in a place called …" He leafed through. "In Cambrils. A property with sixty square metres of floor space, acquired ten years ago."

A factory on sixty square metres?

The notary already spoke further. "It does not have to be an active, producing company. In Spain, there are significant inheritance taxes on residential property. To avoid these taxes, companies are founded and the residential property is transferred to the assets of a company. In the case of inheritance, it is not the property itself that is inherited, but the company. They are no longer subject to inheritance tax. In plain language: The company is probably an auxiliary construction. I assume that you will inherit a flat in the town of Cambrils."

The flat the tattooed girl had talked about! It really existed.

"When did he acquire it?" asked Irene wanly.

The notary flipped back again and gave the year. "In property for ten years, that's good, then there is no concern that the company was set up to avoid inheritance taxes."

Irene gasped for breath. Hubert had kept the existence of this flat from her for ten years. Ten years of lies?

CHAPTER SIX

IRENE DISTRIBUTED COFFEE spoons on saucers. The funeral had been a few days ago now, but the pain still lingered. She felt numb. The cheerful voice of the presenter from the morning show reached her as if through a curtain.

"You really want to go there?" asked Jasmin, taking slices of cheese from a packet and arranging them on a plate for the breakfast buffet.

The coffee spoons clinked when they touched the saucers. Irene paced around the table, rhythmically continuing to distribute the spoons. Clink, clink, clink.

"I'm just saying." Jasmin sounded huffy. "The spring dental conference is coming up."

"Why didn't Olga come?" She had already been absent the other day. "It's ridiculous that we have to prepare breakfast ourselves."

"She's got the flu or something. Someone has to do it. If you go to Spain, I'll be all alone." Jasmin sounded querulous. "And the spring conference is next week. The house full of dentists."

The spoons were on the saucers. Irene took the cups out of the dishwasher. Delicate porcelain cups through which the light shimmered. The smooth material felt good. She placed one after the other on the saucers.

"You know how fussy dentists are." Jasmin did not give up.

"We are two directors. One can be away for a while."

Irene was getting fed up with the discussion. She wouldn't be absent forever. The notary had said something about a Spanish tax number that she would need to dissolve the mysterious company. He had also recommended an advisor who would help her with the bureaucracy and then lost himself in a lecture on Spanish inheritance law.

Meanwhile, the scene at the grave had played over and over again in her mind's eye as the earth slipped from her shovel and hit with a dull sound. How Jasmin clutched her cold hand.

She had only paid attention to the notary's words again when he said, "I'd like to be by the sea again, too."

Even at the cost of losing her spouse, Irene asked herself. Then she pulled herself together. The notary had only wanted to make small talk. In any case, she would soon be at the seaside.

The flat that made up Hubert's company was apparently in a town on the coast. She understood that it could be reached in one or two hours from Barcelona. Not exactly a trip around the world to drop by, get the documents in order and initiate the sale.

The exuberant voice of the radio presenter announced a raffle. Irene reached for the remote control and turned off the radio.

"I have some papers to sign and then I'll be back."

"Surely you can do all that online. The flat ... who knows what it looks like there."

What would it look like there? Like Hubert's office, Irene thought. He never had a knack for interior design.

If she hadn't intervened, her flat would be furnished with fancy but uncomfortable steel furniture and strange modern artworks would hang on exposed concrete walls.

Irene placed more porcelain cups on the saucers. She had reached the tables by the window, which were particularly popular in the morning because the morning sun was shining in. Just make the coffee and everything would be ready for the first early risers.

"Do you really want to look at Pop's love nest?"

Irene slumped down on a chair and hid her face in her hands. She was breathing heavily. 'Love nest'. The words echoed through her head. He had not been there alone. Why hadn't this idea occurred to her? It was also why the pierced one had laid claim to the property. A sharp pain ran through her heart.

Jasmin stepped behind her and stroked her shoulders, massaging the hardened muscles.

"Do you really think so?" Irene noticed how despondent her voice sounded.

"Maybe it really is a commercial enterprise. Who knows what Paps had invested there. He was good with money."

Jasmin was right. Hubert had had a knack for the financial side of things, and in the past few years things had gone steadily upwards. Irene only regretted that he hadn't been more open with her. Why hadn't he told her that he had bought a flat - or a company - in Spain?

CHAPTER SEVEN

IRENE SQUINTED AT THE SEA. The low spring sun cast a glistening trail on the calm water, rippling over the waves. The light blinded Irene. A grey blanket of clouds had hung over Hamburg for the past few months. It hadn't even occurred to her to take her sunglasses when she packed for the flight to Barcelona.

The property held by Daurada Ltda had turned out to be a flat in a holiday complex. She had not seen much of it yet. Last night she had arrived in the dark and fallen onto the sofa, dog-tired. A glance into the bedroom had convinced her that a night on the sofa would be more bearable than in the bed. This morning she had immediately fled the flat again.

Now she was sitting on the terrace of a café, enjoying the light breeze blowing in from the sea. A coffee machine gurgled. A huge, shiny chrome model, as she had noticed with a quick glance at the bar before finding this spot on the terrace.

The sun's rays caressed her skin. She closed her eyes for a moment and enjoyed the warmth. She became aware of her first moment of peace in weeks.

"Here you go". The waiter spoke a few words of German, just as she spoke a few words of Spanish. She remembered more than she thought, even though the stay in Mallorca during her training as a hotel manageress was several decades ago. In front of her now sat a seductive smelling cup of latte with plenty of foam, just the way she loved it. She took a sip and tasted the flavours of vanilla and caramel.

A screech shattered the silence. Irene looked up but couldn't see where the annoying sound came from. From the palm trees that lined the promenade?

"Parrot," said the waiter, who had noticed her glance.

Parrots in Spain?

"Parakeets," said a man sitting at the next table, also drinking coffee, with a newspaper open in front of him. A huge, shaggy dog lay at his feet. "Collared parakeets. They screech unbearably. Pollute everything. They're not from around here."

She peered over at him. He was quite tall, broad-shouldered, wore casual but quality clothes. 'Casual chick', her friend Suzie would have called it. From the tone of his voice, he was also from northern Germany.

"You're not from here either. German?"

Immediately afterwards, Irene regretted her question. She had just heard him speak fluent German. Besides, he had bright blue eyes, his hair was flaxen. Good-looking in a relaxed way. 'I wouldn't push him off the edge of the bed,' would be Suzie's comment. She often only saw a person's appearance. Strange for someone who had immersed herself in yoga and Far Eastern wisdom.

"Yes, but I live here," the stranger replied, as if he had to justify himself.

Irene did not answer. She concentrated on her drink and the magnificent view of the sea. She hadn't come here to get angry about xenophobic remarks, even if they only referred to birds. She had other things to do. The task ahead of her demanded all her strength anyway.

CHAPTER EIGHT

THE WAVES CAME in and out.

Irene could not get enough of the view. She gazed into the blue expanse. The waves were moderately high, not to be compared with the breakers of the North Sea. And yet ... this irregularly even sound ... captivated her. A mild wind blew around her face, carrying scents of rosemary, pine and seaweed.

Each of the waves seemed to carry away one of her worries. Irene had many worries, but the number of waves was infinite. She followed the individual waves as they approached the beach until they broke and turned into white spray. Shouldn't every fifth wave be bigger than the others? Irene started counting, but soon gave up. Every now and then a bigger wave approached, but it was not always the fifth. She could not find any regularity. Nature could not be calculated.

She began to shiver. Despite the blazing sun, the wind kept her cool. She pulled the silk scarf tighter around her neck. A valuable shawl of a traditional French brand that Hubert had given her. "The Hermès scarf holds its value," he had said.

She forbade herself to think about Hubert and continued walking along the beach, enjoying the water on her feet, even more the yielding sand. The movement warmed her up again.

When she looked towards the sun, the sand glittered golden. No wonder the region had been named Costa Daurada, the gilded coast. She had read in the tourist information brochure that splinters of mica slate, on display at the airport, were responsible for the effect. Whatever the reason for the sparkle, it seemed as if gold particles littered the beach. In between, pearly shells, white pebbles and shards of glass abraded by the water stood out, the colour dull yet fascinating.

Irene trudged on, although she had not actually intended to take an extended walk. A few hundred metres in front of her, a man walked his dog. The animal pranced around the man, who kept bending down to pick up and throw a piece of driftwood. The dog ran enthusiastically and retrieved the wood. Otherwise, the beach appeared empty.

In the distance, small chains of hills could be glimpsed, fading towards the horizon. Just then, an aeroplane curved across the sky, leaving a white vapour trail on the blue background. Irene caught herself thinking that she would delay as long as possible before she got back on the plane to Hamburg, despite being urgently needed at the hotel. She pushed the thought away and kept walking. She wanted to look determined.

Small bubbles got stuck in the sand in a fine line at the seashore. Irene was careful not to step on the bubbles, although they were about to burst anyway. A game played according to its own rules.

Despite the cloudless sky, the wind continued to pick up. It carried sand particles that whipped uncomfortably against her calves. She bent down and rolled up her trouser legs again, just enough so that she could still walk barefoot without soaking her trousers.

Her feet were chalky white. No wonder, they hadn't seen the sun all winter. Her nails also needed a pedicure. She straightened up.

At that moment, a gust of wind tore the scarf from her neck. Before she could react, it fluttered away, out to sea. It fell slowly and met a wave that gently lifted it.

Irene saw the bright colours swaying in the water. She ran into the surf, but a slightly higher wave of ice-cold water broke over her jeans. She squealed and ran back onto the firm sand. With each surge, her scarf floated further away. Her heart tightened. Never again would she receive a gift from Hubert. Everything that reminded her of him now was so infinitely precious.

"Porta'l, Fosca!" a dark voice called. The dog she had just seen in the distance plunged into the floods. He was about the size of a sheepdog, but had long, shaggy hair. He paddled with his paws. Soon he seemed to reach the cloth, but whenever he got close, he drifted back again while the waves pulled the cloth out.

"Get him back! He's being dragged away by the current ..."

The man turned to look at her. Now that he was standing right in front of her, she recognised him: the man with the sea-blue eyes who had just been reading the newspaper in the café. He looked at the sea again, at the animal that was eagerly fighting the surf. Then he raised two fingers to his mouth and whistled.

The dog raised its head, turned instantly, and came back to the beach. No sooner had he left the water than he shook himself violently so that drops splashed in all directions. He came running to them, peering guiltily through his forehead fringe with wide eyes. The man bent down, patted and praised the animal. Then he looked up. "I'm sorry."

"It's not so bad," Irene said. She wondered if that was true or just an expression of politeness. One of the last mementos of Hubert was irretrievably lost. The dog shook his shaggy hair again.

Drops of water splashed Irene in the face.

"May I?" The man stepped closer to her, raised his hand, and wiped her chin. Carefully he removed the splashes the dog had shaken in her face. He smiled. As he did so, the lines beside his eyes deepened.

Irene stared at him. Finally, she tore herself away from the sight of those sea-blue eyes. Because she couldn't think of anything better to say, she said: "There's nothing going on here at all, and yet this is a dream beach."

"Spaniards don't go to the sea in winter. Much too cold."

"It's March already."

They trudged side by side through the sand, back towards the marina.

"Yes, but the temperatures are still low. By our standards."

"And you're on the road too, aren't you?"

Irene didn't really care why the man was on the beach, but she had to say something to keep the conversation going.

"My mother is German, I'm probably immune to cold. By the way, my name is Pep." Pep laughed and again those lines formed around his eyes. "I've lived here since I was twenty."

Irene eyed him. How old could he be? The first wrinkles around his eyes, his face tanned - no wonder if he lived here. She could already feel her skin tightening on her nose and cheeks. After the winter she was as pale as cheese. She had to get some sunscreen the next time she went to the supermarket.

"So a local, as it were."

They walked side by side, with Pep always dodging and giving way to her when they came across a clump of seaweed or flotsam that they had to go around.

"It depends on the perspective. The Catalans probably always see me as Aleman, the German, as a foreigner ... I have to live with that." It sounded resigned.

Irene looked up. Apparently not a parrot racist after all, but someone who sat between all chairs. And had come to terms with it. Or struggled with it? She could not tell from his words.

"And the dog needs exercise, for that reason alone I have to go to the beach in all weathers."

The dog seemed to realise that the man was talking about him. He jumped up Irene's leg, seemed to grin at her with his mouth open, his pink tongue hanging out wide.

"May I introduce: Fosca. A Gos catalan, a Catalan herding dog. Belongs to my sister. Most of the time, although it's me who walks him."

Irene looked at the animal kindly, but had no desire to pet the filthy, wet dog. They walked on, Pep said nothing and she enjoyed the moment of walking side by side in silence. The man radiated a kind of inner peace that she missed in herself. Even in normal times.

When they arrived at the marina, they said goodbye and walked away in their own directions. Suddenly it occurred to Irene that she hadn't introduced herself at all. How rude to the man with the sea-blue eyes. She even knew the dog's name: Fosca.

CHAPTER NINE

RUMPLED SHEETS with the duvet squashed at the foot of the bed. Good thing she had slept on the couch in the living room. Tidying up the bedroom after the flight and the train journey had been out of the question. Only the beach walk had given her energy.

Irene stepped up to the window and pulled it open. The flat had been empty for weeks or even months, but she thought she detected an intrusive smell. Cheap perfume mixed with body odours. Mild air flowed in from outside. It carried with it the spicy scent of the pine trees that stood next to the house. The sea shimmered grey-blue.

Irene turned around. She didn't have time to enjoy the view. This place urgently needed tidying up. She grabbed the roll of grey-black plastic bags, tore one off and shook it open. Then she threw everything into it that was on the bedside table: a packet of handkerchiefs, a pen ... Wait, Hubert's reading glasses. One of the many pairs of glasses from the drugstore that he kept misplacing. The glasses also went into the bin bag. Hubert wouldn't need them anymore and they were too cheap to donate to an old people's home.

Irene opened the top drawer and gasped. Condom packets in all colours, a tube of lubricant and something snakelike formed from silicone. She pulled out the entire drawer of the bedside cabinet, pulled the rubbish bag over it and shook it. She let the empty drawer sink to the floor.

Irene sat down on the bed. This was beyond her. With her foot, she nudged a tiny pair of panties lying on the bedside rug. In the past few years Hubert had rarely deigned to caress her, let alone wanted sex. She presumed it was normal at their age and consoled herself with cheap romance novels, which she devoured as long as her work at the hotel gave her time for it. Here, however, Hubert had obviously maintained a real love nest. She would clear it out, clean it thoroughly and then sell it. Out of sight, out of mind. There would be enough interested parties.

The flat was located in a complex that had obviously been built for holiday guests, according to the land register in the early 1980s. The spacious living room with the floor-to-ceiling window offered a fantastic view of the sea, as the flat was on the third floor with a view over the outer wall of the apartment complex. The balcony offered space for a small table with two chairs, and a folded laundry rack stood in one corner. The living room included an American kitchen with a counter. Of course, Hubert had not cooked, but had gone to one of the restaurants.

Irene had no desire to visit a restaurant alone. The smaller bedroom she now sat in had a window facing the mountains. Better than one facing the courtyard with the swimming pool, Irene thought. A modern bathroom and a tiny room that served as a storeroom completed the flat.

Hubert had chosen the flat carefully. In summer, noise from the pool might echo up to the other flats. Irene imagined how it would look if she put some plants on the balcony. Oleander would be perfect for this climate. And this modern leather sofa would have to give way to a cosy couch with lots of cushions. Dirty pink would fit wonderfully.

She decided to get new bed linen first. The thought of sleeping in the same sheets Hubert and that tramp ... choked her. She escaped from the bedroom into the great room, opened the balcony door and stepped out. Breathed in the salty sea air deeply.

She heard a rattle. It was coming from the other side of the balcony partition. Each of the two flats had a balcony divided by a pane of frosted glass. The rattling repeated itself. It sounded like a moan, but filled with pain. She stepped up to the partition, stood on tiptoe and peered over. What she saw made her shiver. A stark-naked guy stuck his bum out at her. He groaned audibly. Then she heard a sweet voice: "One more inhale and exhale loudly." The fellow rasped again. "From the downward facing dog move forward into the plank ..." The man's muscles tensed, he slid forward into a kind of push-up.

Irene withdrew. She had seen enough. The neighbour was not rattling, but practising yoga. Naked. On the balcony. That was his right, she reflected. It was her fault for peeping over the cover. She sat down at the little table again. The coffee no longer tasted good. A feeling of loneliness overwhelmed her. No one cared whether she ate breakfast or not. How it tasted to her. In general, she had lost her appetite. She hid her face in her hands and cried. For the first time since the funeral, she let the tears run free.

CHAPTER TEN

"THROW HER OUT ALREADY!" Montse leafed listlessly through a gossip magazine. For months she had been nagging him, telling him to finally do the deed. The dog lay at her feet, watching Pep through the shag that fell down his forehead. After the long walk on the beach, he was relaxed.

"You know very well that she is pregnant."

Montse pursed her mouth. "That's no reason."

His sister wore a tight top with colourful harem trousers. She had dark eyes and frizzy black hair. She always complained that she had inherited her looks from her Catalan father. If she had been tall and blue-eyed like Pep, she would have been coveted as an exotic beauty in Catalonia. But as it was, she was just one Morena among many.

"Surely I can't throw a pregnant woman out on the street, even if it's my ex."

"But Ana can go to Barcelona every morning, work, fuck her new Casanova and come back in the evening? She's not too pregnant for that?"

Pep cringed inwardly at his sister's bluntness. Even as a child, she had always blurted out what no one else said. The legacy of her German mother, presumably.

"The rents are astronomical in Barcelona."

"Cariño, Ana's just too comfortable. Why doesn't she move in with the Casanova?" With one bare foot she stroked Fosca's back, who then closed his eyes with pleasure.

"Because he's still studying and lives with his parents? She's got herself a toyboy."

Montse grunted. "Madonna is supposed to have a younger lover too."

That hurt. Pep, at 47, felt like a grandfather. Ana was nine years younger than him. Did she think of him as an old fart? When they had fallen in love, she had always protested that the age difference didn't bother her. And now she dated a student. Okay, he worked on his doctoral thesis, did that still count as studying? Anyway, he was in his early thirties and only five years younger than Ana. Even if Madonna or other rock stars kept some kind of toyboys, it was far from common here in Spain for the woman to be older than the man. In any case, he knew of no example.

"Luisa is also older than Hanna."

"They're lesbians, for heaven's sake."

Montse looked up from her magazine. "So what? It just goes to show, one of them has to be older if they weren't born on the same day."

The discussion went round in circles. Pep wondered whether he should tell Montse about the German he had met on the beach. This quiet woman who seemed somehow melancholic, but attracted him nonetheless.

Fosca got up, yawned and stretched. Then she nudged him on the knee. She wanted to go out again, run and romp.

"Haven't you had enough yet?" Pep turned back to Montse: "If I take the dog today, will you make tortilla for the Xiquets' meeting?" The 'boys', as they called themselves, were men and women dedicated to the Castells' hobby: human towers.

"Is the season starting again?"

"Yes, Xavi got everyone together." His friend Xavi had been the president of the community which cultivated this Catalan custom for many years.

"Deal, if you bring Fosca back tonight, you can pick up the tortilla."

In an elegant way, she had left her dog in his care for the day.

CHAPTER ELEVEN

THE COFFEE HAD GONE COLD. She gulped it down anyway. Then she left the balcony and went into the bathroom. From the mirror, a fifty-one-year-old woman with red tears in her eyes looked back at her. She averted her eyes and splashed water on her face.

She stepped up to the kitchen counter and opened the fridge. Canned milk, mustard, a packet of margarine, two bottles of beer. She had to go shopping. Beforehand, she called Jasmin to see if everything went well at the hotel. But her daughter did not answer. She was probably too busy.

Irene grabbed the cloth bag hanging on a hook next to the door and explored the surroundings. She soon found a small supermarket. She picked up some basic foodstuffs. When she came back from shopping, she met a man at the front door who seemed to be about her age. He looked athletic, but not muscular. He was carrying a large wicker basket with a leek sticking out of it, a cauliflower and a whole lot of artichokes.

Together they climbed the stairs. The man stopped at the door next to hers, turned to her and held out his hand. "Karl is my name, so here they call me Carlos. Did you buy the flat from Hubert?"

He smiled kindly at her.

Irene blushed to the roots of her hair. Carlos must be the yogi from the balcony next door. This morning she had stared at his bare bottom. She felt herself turning red as a beetroot. Her mouth opened automatically and she reeled off some pleasantries. She rummaged frantically for her key.

Then she felt ridiculous. She had done nothing wrong. And Karl - Carlos - didn't even know that she had watched him naked during his early morning exercise. Her gaze wandered down his body. He was wearing shorts, his legs were hairy. He wore sandals, but with white socks. Not the latest fashion. Irene was glad, however, that he was clothed at all.

She said noncommittally, "The flat needs renovating." Then she blurted out, "What are you doing with all those artichokes?" Immediately she regretted her question. It was none of her business. Let him eat artichokes from morning till night, maybe that was part of the yogi lifestyle.

Carlos kindly replied: "They are in season and very cheap. I'm making a salad; would you like to join me? Come on!"

Irene felt relieved not to have to sit alone in the flat again. The lawyer who would support her in dealing with the authorities had only given her an appointment in the afternoon. She followed Carlos.

His flat had the same layout as hers, but in a mirror image. In the hallway, the bathroom and bedroom went off to the left instead of to the right like hers. They entered the living room.

The bright and modern look at Irene's had been replaced by a grandmother's parlour. Dark, antique furniture with lots of cushions and doilies. An oil painting of a ship on the high seas hung above the sofa. She would have expected this living room to be in Hamburg rather than Cambrils.

Carlos noticed her astonishment. "You need a little reminder of home, don't you?" he said. He heaved his bags onto the kitchen sideboard, put vegetables in the fridge and placed fruit in a bowl. Wonderfully fragrant oranges. Then he piled the artichokes on the table and reached for a knife.

Irene watched in suspense as he cut up the vegetables and cut away the inedible parts. In the end, the huge pile of artichokes had turned into a small bowl of artichoke hearts. "I soak them in lemon water so they don't turn brown," Carlos explained.

Irene nodded. She also treated apple pieces for the cake in this way, so they didn't become unsightly.

Carlos put on water to boil the artichokes. "This is going to take a moment. Would you like some wine? I have here ..."

"Isn't it too early for wine?" A glance at her watch showed: it was barely twelve o'clock.

"Only as an aperitif." He grabbed a bottle from a well-stocked wine rack next to the fridge. "Blanc de Blancs, a very light, fresh white, that will do." Carlos handled a bottle opener, poured and handed her a glass. "Cheers! To good neighbours!"

"Cheers." She didn't have to tell him that she wouldn't be moving in.

"At the moment everything is still quiet and still, the season starts from Easter. That's when most of the other flats are occupied."

"What were the people like in my flat?" Irene would have liked to take the question back immediately. But now she had blurted it out.

"The lawyer? He came about three or four times a year. With his mistress, if you ask me."

"Oh?"

"Yes, strange couple. An architect, also from Hamburg, as far as I know. We're already a small colony here. North Germans in the southern sun." He smiled.

"And with a lover?" Irene was pained by the question, the answer would be even more painful, but she couldn't help herself.

"A young girl with colourful hair and piercings. The style didn't suit him at all. You'd think an architect would have something with his secretary, the classic, cool blonde with a model figure. But no, Hubert always came with a black-clad creature with a lot of metal on her face."

Irene thought of the secretary of the architect's office, whom the old Backhoff had hired. She was not at all the type of a classic mistress. Too old, too stiff, she thought bitterly. Just as I had become too old for Hubert at some point.

"Sometimes the woman came here alone, then she buried herself in books and studied," Carlos babbled on. "Is everything all right in the flat?"

"It needs cleaning." That must have come across as arrogant. As if she was too refined for that. But there was no way she would bring this love nest into a habitable condition herself.

"You're looking for cleaning help?" Carlos didn't bat an eyelid. "No problem, I'll send Araceli over. I do the caretaking here, for which the house community pays me a small fee. If there's anything wrong, you come to me. I do small repairs myself, I used to be a plumber."

He gave her a friendly nod. "Right after dinner I'll call Araceli, she'll clean up, you won't recognise the place."

He toasted her and smiled kindly.

She smiled back, but her thoughts were elsewhere.

Carlos proved to be a charming conversationalist and a good cook. They chatted in a relaxed manner. Finally, Irene said goodbye and went back to the flat next door.

As soon as she opened the door, she knew that she didn't just need cleaning help. The couch had been moved away from the wall, cushions lay on the floor. Looking closer, the living room was also a mess. The drawers of a chest of drawers were open. Irene ventured a look into the bedroom. There, the drawers of the bedside cabinets had been torn out. The thief had come too late, Irene thought, because she had dumped the contents of the drawers in a rubbish bag yesterday and disposed of them. But whoever had broken in had certainly not been looking for sex toys.

She went back to the flat door, opened it and examined the lock. No scratch marks, even the door frame was intact. Had the pierced woman been here? Rummaged through everything looking for something valuable? She had claimed that she had a key to the flat.

What was she looking for? Was something missing? Irene let her gaze wander, but could not determine whether she was missing anything. She had her purse and mobile phone with her. Apart from that, she didn't think there were any valuables in the flat.

Irene turned and knocked on Carlos' door, who opened immediately.

"Forgotten what?"

"I need a locksmith. The front door lock needs to be changed." She did not say that someone had broken in.

"No problem. I'll call Juan."

CHAPTER TWELVE

A STOCKY MAN in blue overalls was fiddling with the lock. He smiled uncertainly at Irene and continued his work.

Irene had taken refuge in the café on the beach promenade while Carlos had activated his helpers. Now the flat smelled of the lemon aroma of a floor cleaner. Araceli had cleaned, and thoroughly. The layer of dust had disappeared from the furniture, the kitchen shone and the windows sparkled with cleanliness. The view of the sea was unclouded. She lost herself in the sight of the blue expanse.

The whirring of a cordless screwdriver called them back to the moment. Juan fastened the fitting of the lock. Irene wondered if she should offer him something to drink. She took two glasses from the cupboard, opened the fridge and reached for the Coke bottle. The Coke would taste even better with ice. She opened the flap of the icebox. Sure enough, there she found an ice maker, next to it a packet of spinach. Lost in thought, she broke some ice cubes out of the plastic tray and let them slide into the Coke.

Spinach? Unlike her, Hubert had never liked the vegetable. When she prepared spinach, she had to cook something extra for him. Was his floozy into greens? All the young girls were vegans these days. She took the package. Would the contents still be edible? When she turned it over in her hands to look for a best-before date, she saw that the box was already torn open. She opened the flap.

Banknotes. Instead of a frozen block of pureed spinach leaves, notes came towards her. Fifties, hundreds, five-hundreds. A thick stack of money in the box of a packet of frozen food.

Irene suddenly felt Juan's eyes on her back. Hectically, she stuffed the notes back into the package and pushed it back into the icebox, which she closed with a bang. Then she turned and held out a glass of Coke to the locksmith, in which three harmless ice cubes were floating: "Te apetece una Coca Cola?"

Embarrassed, the man accepted the lemonade, drank in hasty draughts. Then he pointed to the lock, put two brand new keys in her hand. He pulled out his mobile phone, tapped away on it and showed Irene the display of a calculator, the result field of which showed a ridiculously small sum. She took her purse out of her handbag and gave him his wages, rounding it up with a generous tip. The man thanked her and left.

I wonder if he spotted the notes from the fridge. But she had turned her back on him. Her body had probably blocked the view of the pile of money.

Irene downed her Coke, went to the door and locked it twice. The new key still hooked a little.

Then she opened the icebox again, took out the spinach packet and took out the notes. She sat down at the dining table and counted. At one hundred and twenty thousand she got confused and gave up.

Where did Hubert get so much cash? Irene gulped. She had never seen such a quantity of notes at once. She needed peace and quiet to think about the find. Only one thing was clear: the treasure couldn't stay in the fridge, because Juan might have been watching her. She had to think of a better hiding place.

CHAPTER THIRTEEN

PEP WATCHED ATTENTIVELY as Irene followed the words of Doctor Enrique Palau Rivera. The senior had built up the Gestoria, he had good contacts up to the highest circles of the Catalan regional government. To this day, the gentleman with the carefully coiffed white hair insisted on receiving all new clients personally, only then leaving the case to one of his staff.

Irene's gaze slid to him again and again. So she had recognised him, just as he had recognised her. The attractive woman from the beach. He smiled at her.

However, she concentrated closely on the words of Don Enrique, who had learned the German language in an elite boarding school in Switzerland, but who expressed himself somewhat awkwardly. Now he tried to explain that the Spanish bureaucracy was so complex that it had spawned its own profession, that of the gestor. The gestor took over all the official procedures for his clients, from the application for a building permit to the tax return to more complex cases such as the transfer of a company to an heiress.

Irene was playing with a biro in her hands. The slender woman was about his age, Don Enrique estimated. He would see her details when they opened the file. She was tastefully dressed and held herself straight.

Yet she seemed depressed. Hardly surprising since she's just widowed, he scolded himself. Now, on top of that, she faced a tangled mess of bureaucracy, and Spanish-type bureaucracy at that.

"... our partner Josep Folch i Bosch will guide you through the process." He was just aware that Don Enrique had handed him the floor. Everyone looked at him expectantly.

He cleared his throat, glanced at the notebook in front of him. "It's about the company Daurada Ltda. or rather the property of this company." He wondered if his client was aware that this company had only been set up as a cover for real estate ownership. He read off the address. Not premium, but still a good location. A small flat in a complex near the marina.

"I want to sell the flat," said Irene Hansen. "How do I have to proceed? Can you help me?"

Of course he could. He would have loved to take her in his arms and comfort her. Where did he get this idea?

Aloud he said: "You need a Spanish tax number. You have to apply for it in Madrid." He tried not to let his dislike of the central government come through. "That takes about eight weeks."

"Eight weeks?"

"Yes, we can pressure them for it. On average, it takes more like three months. You can also apply for the number in Germany at the Spanish embassy, but that would take even longer. I would be happy to get you the tax number. In the meantime, we can already hire an estate agent to show the flat to interested parties."

"I thought you were the estate agent?"

Apparently, she had not followed Don Enrique's explanations. "We here at the Gestoria are lawyers, but we work with a network of tax advisors, accountants and other professionals. Our estate agent would put the flat on the market. However, once you've sold the flat, the limited company still exists - we're also happy to help you with any dissolution of the business."

The widow's mouth was agape. She probably had the feeling that he was trying to talk her into an unnecessary service. So he explained: "Spanish bureaucracy is so complicated that even most locals don't face it themselves. Those who can afford it hire a Gestoria to do the paper-work. They save themselves filling out forms and standing in line for hours."

Irene nodded surrendered.

"Are you sure you want to sell the flat? It's a good value investment. Prices on the coast are rising again after a brief dip during the pandemic."

"Yes, I'm certain."

"You could rent it out. An agency would take over the management for a commission." Selling the flat would make no economic sense. Did the Hamburg woman need money? She seemed well off. She was also expecting an inheritance. "You wouldn't have to worry about the flat, you'd just get the rental income. Here on the Costa Daurada, we have an occupancy rate of eighty per cent on an annual average."

"I'm selling the flat." Suddenly, Pep recognised Irene as a tough busi-nesswoman. His first impression of a somewhat coy, insecure woman had been completely wrong. His curiosity about her personality rose. What was the cagey German hiding behind her armour?

CHAPTER FOURTEEN

THE RING TONE SOUNDED. Irene hopped back and forth. Hopefully Suzie wasn't in the middle of a yoga class. Although ... it was probably too late in the evening for that. Had her friend already gone to bed?

Finally she took the call.

Irene exhaled. She hadn't even noticed that she had been holding her breath. Suzie's throaty voice made her relax. They exchanged a few words of greeting, then Irene told her about the money she had found.

Suzie laughed at the top of her lungs. "Spend it!"

She always saw things so simply. Irene couldn't just spend money that didn't belong to her. Or was it part of her inheritance?

"And you say someone broke in?"

Irene described the condition of the flat. "They were looking for the money."

"Who's them?"

"I have no idea."

Irene had tried not to think about it, but involuntarily the image of the pierced young woman came before her eyes. "Besides, they supposedly had a key. There were no signs of forced entry."

"True again." Suzie was silent for a while, quite against her habit.

Irene told about the helpful neighbour, but kept quiet about the walk on the beach with Pep. She knew what Suzie would comment on anyway. 'If you like him, why don't you start something with him?' As if Hubert hadn't died recently. As if he wasn't missing at every moment.

Don't be a chicken, she scolded herself. How could you miss Hubert when you rarely saw him, and you were always at the hotel. You obviously hardly knew him, considering what you have found out in the last few days.

"I envy you," Suzie just said.

"Why is that?"

"You're in the sunny south having adventures."

Irene could do without that kind of adventure.

Besides, she had just lost her husband. There was a hole in her life, a huge hole. Sometimes Suzie was just insensitive. Still, she was glad to have a friend she could call at any time. They chatted a bit more, then someone rang Suzie's doorbell.

She was probably receiving a guy she had picked up somewhere, Irene thought. Then she reminded herself not to be envious. She herself would never get involved with a man as lightly as Suzie, who was now hurriedly taking her leave.

No sooner had she finished talking than Jasmin called. Yes, she was fine. Yes, everything was running smoothly at the hotel. Yes, the online portals had increased their commission again, but with the occupancy at this time of year, that was not a problem for the time being.

"Our calculation is tight anyway." Irene counted in her head how much they would lose per booking if these sharks wanted larger percentages.

"We are raising prices."

Jasmin had learned a few things at hotel management school, but competitive costing did not seem to be one of them. Irene resolved to check the annual budget as soon as she returned to Hamburg. Maybe she could find a cheaper electricity provider. "We can't charge more than other comparable houses."

"Mum, don't worry, I have a plan."

CHAPTER FIFTEEN

SHE HAD SLEPT MORE PEACEFULLY that night because of the security provided by her new lock. Her thoughts revolved around the appointment with the Gestor. She would probably meet the man with the sea-blue eyes again, because they still had a lot to do before the flat could be sold.

She sipped a latte. Having breakfast on a terrace right on the beach is something you could get used to, she thought, gazing out at the expanse of the sea. Today there were hardly any waves to be seen, it was almost windless. A blue-grey mass of water lazily sloshed onto the beach.

Her mobile phone rang. Did Jasmin need help? In a hotel, something could go wrong at any time. She remembered the Japanese man who had taken a shower so hot that the fire alarm had gone off. The failure of the laundry service. And the suicide at Christmas.

She frantically dug the phone out of her handbag. It was not Jasmin, an unknown Hamburg number was on the display. "Yes?"

"Chief Inspector Volker Kroeger here, Hamburg Crime Investigation Unit. I need to ask you a few more questions, when can you come by?"

Hubert was cremated and buried, what did the policeman want to know from her? She ran over her schedule. "Next week? Wednesday, maybe?"

She sensed the commissioner's displeasure even before he said, "No, please come by today or tomorrow. The address ..."

"I'm afraid I can't, I'm abroad."

"Abroad?"

"I'm in Spain."

"Then I will ask my questions now, please make sure we are undisturbed for a while. I would email you the minutes later."

Protocol? That sounded formal. Before she could think about it further, she heard Kroeger say, "Where were you at the time of your husband's passing?"

What was the significance of that? "I was at home."

"Can anyone attest to that?"

She thought about it. She had waited for Hubert on Friday evening; when he didn't come, she had gone to bed. On Saturday morning, Jasmin had come for breakfast. She told Kroeger that too.

He seemed to be taking notes, because it took a moment before he spoke again.

"Did your husband have any enemies?"

"Why are you asking now? Hasn't the file been closed for a long time?"

"Please just answer my questions. Did your husband have any opponents? Professional rivals?" The commissioner spoke slowly and calmly.

"What enemies would an architect from a prestigious Hamburg office have? The idea is absurd. I don't know what you want from me. Hubert is buried, you can close your case."

"Unfortunately, we have to assume that it was not an accident."

"He crashed the car, didn't he?"

"The forensic medicine has provided a final report. The examination was complex because of the condition of the body, but the findings are conclusive. We found a gunshot wound."

"A bullet wound?" She felt like a parrot, but for the life of her she couldn't help repeating the police officer's words.

"Yes, someone shot him in the chest. If it's any consolation: they killed him instantly." He paused. "He wouldn't have known about the accident. Or the fire."

Was that supposed to reassure her? Her thoughts raced. Hubert shot dead? Surely the officer was mistaken.

"What makes you think he was shot? That's absurd."

" The prosecutor released the body because no further examinations were needed. Although they released the forensic report days ago, the file remained abandoned for some time because my colleague went on parental leave. Now I have inherited the case, and I have some questions for you."

"Was Hubert mixed up in something criminal?" That was the only explanation she could think of in a flash.

"We don't know at this stage. Our investigation is still ongoing. How was your marriage?"

Irene's heart tightened. That was none of this policeman's business.

"Good," she said tonelessly. Was that a lie now?

"There is a witness statement that speaks of your husband having a female companion in the car. Who could that have been? Did he perhaps pick up a hitchhiker?"

Irene almost laughed. Hubert certainly didn't pick up hitchhikers. A thought flashed through her mind, but she dismissed it immediately. "Can you describe the woman or send a photo? Maybe I know her by sight."

"Unfortunately, we do not have a description. The person is said to have had very light hair, that's the only thing we know. And it was probably a woman or a very petite slim man with long hair. Our guess is more likely a woman. Can you help us with that?"

Irene would have liked to end the call. The situation got worse and worse. She knew a petite woman with platinum blonde hair. She just didn't know her name. Had Hubert's mistress killed him?

CHAPTER SIXTEEN

SHE OPENED another sachet of sugar and stirred the contents into her coffee. The café had become her second home. She just didn't feel like sitting in the flat and waiting. The estate agent didn't have time for her until tomorrow, Pep from the Gestoria was going to get papers for her to sign. It was still too early to get a ticket for the return flight.

Her phone beeped and vibrated on the table. A message from Suzie.

How are you? A smiley face followed.

I'm fine, she wrote back.

A smiley face with a kissing mouth popped up. *Be glad you're in the south, cold and grey here.*

Irene squinted into the sun. It was pleasant here on the café's wind-protected terrace. Nevertheless, she pulled her cardigan tighter around her shoulders.

She knew should not discuss the topic in a chat, but it didn't stop her typing: *Bad news. Hubert had allegedly been shot.*

It took time to get an answer.

Who says so?

Police.

Suzie sent an emoji with wide eyes.

Then the phone rang. "You poor thing, that's terrible."

Irene was glad to hear Suzie's voice. Suddenly she realised how much she missed her friend.

"What happened?"

Irene repeated what the police officer had told her. She could almost see Suzie shaking her head in disbelief. "That Hubert met his end like this, I can't believe it."

"Neither can I. He must have been involved in something. You don't just get ..." The word 'shot' did not cross her lips.

"Maybe it's a mix-up." Suzie placated.

Irene knew that wasn't true. The cash hidden in the freezer could not have an innocent origin. And someone had obviously broken into the flat and searched it. And the fact that Hubert had paid for the flat in cash. A slush fund, presumably. Money whose existence she hadn't suspected or known about.

"It might be," she said evasively. Under no circumstances did she want to discuss her husband's dubious activities on the phone.

Suzie did not elaborate on the thought. Instead she said, "I always thought you were happy."

"That's what I thought too." She had rarely seen Hubert lately, but she had blamed that on all the work he had been doing in the well-run architect's office. And she herself had been fully focused on the hotel. To distract myself? Involuntarily, a sigh escaped her.

"You have to think about yourself now. Are you doing the yoga exercises I showed you?"

"Yes." Irene lied listlessly.

"They help to start the day in a positive mood," cautioned Suzie, who guessed Irene wanted to avoid a discussion. "Yoga is more than a physical exercise. You mustn't neglect yourself now."

Irene burst into tears. it seemed to her that her whole life had been a lie. A marriage built on sand. Hubert had had a mistress, vast sums of cash of unknown origin and a secret flat in Spain - a bit much all at once. Plus the horrible idea of the accident, which apparently wasn't one. She sobbed until she could no longer breathe.

"My dear!" Suzie spoke soothingly to her.

Irene noticed that the waiter was watching her from the bar. She rummaged a packet of paper tissues out of her handbag, fumbled one out and blew her nose.

"You know what, I'm coming over to see you. I don't want you to be alone right now," Suzie said.

"You don't have to."

"Possibly, but it can't hurt either."

"And the studio?"

"My assistant Melina is taking over for the time being. She has settled in well here in the last few months."

"Okay."

The idea of having her friend by her side and being able to discuss things with her gave Irene a boost. She blew her nose again, this time more determinedly.

"I'll book a flight right away and send you the details."

Shortly afterwards, the mobile beeped again. Suzie had found a cheap offer and she would come the day after tomorrow.

Irene texted back telling her that she would pick her up at Barcelona airport. It was the least she could do, she thought. After all, she had the rental car.

Suzie ended the chat with a symbol of a raised thumb and another kissing mouth. Then the mobile rang and showed Jasmin's number, but Irene was too exhausted to take the call. She didn't want her daughter to notice how unhappy she was. She would call back later.

CHAPTER SEVENTEEN

"THROW THEM OUT ALREADY!" Xavi spun around himself while Pep held on to his sash. "You should have done it a long time ago."

The metre-long belt had to be wrapped tightly around his waist to withstand the high stresses of building a human tower. These Catalan human towers, known as castells, had been recognised by Unesco as a Heritage of Humanity. A highly lively culture had evolved. Even in the smallest villages there were associations, so-called collas, which competed with each other to see who could build the highest and best human tower. Even if the masterpieces only lasted a few seconds in their completion before they were hastily dismantled again.

"Don't you remember what we agreed back then? Never start anything with a tourist..."

"... she leaves and forgets you," Pep completed the sentence they had recited to each other over and over again as teenagers while they had stared at the bare-chested blondes from the north on the beach.

He handed the end of the belt cloth to Xavi, who took a deep breath and tucked it under the bottom layer of the sash. Now the belt was so tight that a full-grown man could anchor his foot in it and climb up over his back to the next level of the human tower.

"Been a long time."

"I hear you're going out with an Alemana." Xavi spoke calmly and firmly. As Cap de Colla, who directed the construction of the human towers, he had a natural authority.

"Oh!" Not for the first time, Pep wondered at the speed with which rumours spread. And with which a walk on the beach turned into an affair.

"My mother's hairdresser heard it from Montse, so it must be true. Is she hot?"

"Well, first of all, it's my client, not my girlfriend. Secondly, we met by chance on the beach. And thirdly, it's none of your fucking business whether she's hot or not." Without meaning to, his voice rose more and more.

"So, you fancy her." Xavi grinned. Then he made defensive motions with his hands. "Be cool!"

Pep snorted.

"Do you want me to check her out for you?"

Xavi alluded to his father's profession as Mossos d'Esquadra. As an officer of the Catalan National Police, there were ways for him to check up on a person. Xavi was supposed to have followed in his footsteps, but he had chosen a different career as a civil servant - at the post office.

"She's a harmless German. I'm helping her sell a flat she inherited from her husband." How strange that sounded! Normally one would say 'she wants to sell the flat after her husband's death'. Now it struck him that Irene had phrased it differently. As if a stranger had unexpectedly bequeathed her the flat.

"She's a widow?" Xavi interrupted his thoughts. "Then get rid of Ana as soon as possible."

"I don't want anything from her. You know I'd never start anything with a tourist." His friend was getting on his nerves.

Xavi suddenly became serious. He slapped him on the back. "Alemana or not, it's important that you're happy. This thing with Ana has got to you."

Did Xavi just give him carte blanche to hook up with a foreigner?

One by one, the other members of the Colla arrived. The men slapped Xavi on the back in greeting, the women gave kisses on the cheeks. Together they had repaired the building that the Cambrils municipality had given to the Colla. The roof was renewed and part of it was raised so that there was enough space for the castells, where up to eight people stood piled on top of each other.

There were two bars set into the wall, shoulder-width apart. A woman held on to the bars while her daughter crawled up her back and stood on her shoulders. Just as nimbly as she had climbed up, she slid back down her mother's body. Pep had always assumed that men were more drawn to the Castellers, but tonight there were as many women as men, of all ages. A toddler was also there, crawling among the people and being cuddled on all sides.

When enough members were gathered, the serious part of the training began. Xavi lined up four men who had a similar build - stocky with broad shoulders - in a square. He carefully measured the distances between them with outstretched arms and pushed them around a little until they formed a regular square. They had placed their arms on the shoulders of their respective neighbours.

One of them had turned up his jacket collar and put the tips in his mouth. He bit the tip of the collar, on the one hand to protect his teeth in case the tower collapsed, and on the other hand so that the jacket wouldn't slip; it was supposed to give the others a good grip. That was how Xavi had explained it when Pep had once asked about it.

Now two women stepped behind the men, got their feet into the sashes on their backs and climbed onto their shoulders, supporting each other. Two of the younger children, perhaps eight or nine years old, deftly pushed themselves up the tower of men. The remaining members of the colla stood around the outside of the castell, supporting the others. This was the so-called pinya, as even Pep knew, who had little interest in the sport. However, since Castellers performed at all the popular festivals in Catalonia, he was used to the sight. Nevertheless, the acrobatic performance was always fascinating. With bated breath, he watched as a child of about six climbed up the tower. At least this girl was wearing a helmet. At the top, she straightened up and stretched one hand upwards. This sign, the 'little wing', indicated the completion of the tower. Then, without hesitation but in no hurry, the child slid back down to the ground. The others followed until the tower was completely dismantled. Pep exhaled again.

Everyone clapped their hands.

Pep used the moment to say goodbye to Xavi. He was sure he would never join the Colla, even though his friend spoke highly of the group's cohesion and friendship. For him, so much physical contact with strangers, well, with people who were not part of his family, was unimaginable. There was probably more German in him than he wanted to admit, he thought. A real southerner wouldn't mind crawling over other bodies or serving as their foundation.

CHAPTER EIGHTEEN

SHE YAWNED. She had tossed and turned for hours all night. When she finally fell asleep, a nightmare had tormented her. Even now, the images ran through her head: a gun pointed at Hubert's head. Hubert wrecking his car and hitting a tree. A young woman with metal piercings on her face, kissing Hubert passionately.

She shook her head. Then she turned her attention to the young man who gave her a professional smile. His teeth shone white, he must have had them bleached regularly. She couldn't care less, she called herself to order. "Was it you who arranged the purchase of the flat for my husband?" she asked.

The estate agent frowned. He could imagine what her marriage would have been like if she asked him that question. But she didn't care. She was sick of fooling herself. She wanted to know everything. Since when Hubert had been acting behind her back. Why he had bought this flat. How much money he had spent on it instead of helping her renovate the hotel. And what this mistress was all about. Bitter truths, but she wanted to face them. She had a right to know everything.

The estate agent leafed through a pile of papers. "In the land register it is recorded that the flat was acquired ten years ago, I wasn't working here then."

Surely, he had been in school at that time. A thought crossed her mind. "Is there another person in the land register?" Had Hubert registered his mistress? But then she wouldn't have to fight for the inheritance, would she? Maybe she owned a share of the property?

"I'm sorry to disappoint you, you're not on the land register."

The estate agent had to assume that she had not really communicated with her husband. Which was close to the truth. But her question had not yet been answered. Irene asked again: "Hubert was the only one listed in the land register?

"The flat is owned by Daurada Ltda. which in Spanish corresponds to a limited liability company, i.e. a GmbH. Its sole owner is Hubert Hansen. The purchase price was two hundred thousand euros, which was paid in cash."

Irene gasped. Two hundred thousand euros in cash? Was that even allowed? She thought of the notes stored in the spinach packet in the fridge. She couldn't think of a better hiding place.

"In cash?" she breathed.

The broker slid back and forth on his chair, pushed the glasses up on his nose. They were a flamboyant, angular model that at least gave his chubby face some shape. "That is not uncommon in this country. Many foreigners in particular pay cash for real estate. Also, I would like to point out to you that usually only part of the purchase price is securitised."

"What does that mean?" She blinked in confusion.

He moved on the chair again. "The purchase sum was certainly higher. If things went as they often do, part of the amount was handed over directly to the seller without being notarised before the notary. Both sides thus save on incidental costs, taxes and so on. You can assume that the flat was about thirty percent more expensive. Even then, you couldn't get a flat at the marina for two hundred thousand euros, which is a sought-after location."

A stab went through her heart. On a rough estimate, the flat must have cost around three hundred thousand euros, plus notary fees, purchase taxes and probably an estate agent's fee. Money that Hubert had possessed and about which she had not known anything. Tears welled up in her eyes. She forced them back.

"Thank you for the information. I would like to sell, and as soon as possible. My Spanish tax number has been applied for. Can you do something until it is issued?"

The estate agent put on a professional smile. "Of course, we can already acquire interested parties. First of all, I'd like to take a look at the property to determine the current price. Survey the condition of the building, you know. Then I need access to show the flat. Just leave the key here."

He obviously assumed that she would now fly to the airport and back to Germany. Or did he think she was staying in a hotel? She hesitated.

There were three keys for the new lock, she only had one with her. The estate agent could get his copy when he came to look at it. She glanced at her calendar. Actually, she had time to show him the flat now.

But something was holding her back. The mornings in the café, the walks on the beach ... she could savour these for a few more days before returning to grey Hamburg and throwing herself into the stress of the hotel. With Hubert's inheritance, it had to be possible for her and Jasmin to carry out the long overdue renovations. She absolutely had to call Jasmin and discuss how they were going to proceed.

Then the memory of a pair of sea-blue eyes slipped into her thoughts.

"You can come by my place on Saturday," she told the estate agent. That secured her another weekend in Cambrils. They agreed on a time. Relieved to have made a decision, Irene left the office.

CHAPTER NINETEEN

THE DOORS SLID open and a crowd of people came out. Irene looked for her friend's flaming red hair, but did not spot her. She sweated. The airport felt suffocating. Other people were crowding around her, waiting for arrivals. Next to her, a young woman in fancy dress held a sign saying *Mr Müller*. A clip on her blazer identified her as an employee of a tourist chain. Hopefully she did not know how many Müllers there were in the world.

Again the doors slid open, again people dragged their wheeled suitcases out of the gate. A man next to her broke away from the group of waiting people and walked towards a woman with a large backpack. He handed her a rose. She fell around his neck. The two held each other for a while.

Irene felt a stab in her heart. How long had it been since Hubert had surprised her with flowers?

Someone next to her cleared their throat.

She looked up.

A tall man had his bright blue eyes fixed on her and was smiling cautiously.

"Pep! What a surprise!" She suddenly became aware of the sweat on her forehead. Her clothes were wrinkled from the ride. She would have preferred to hide in a mouse hole.

"I'm picking up a colleague, who are you waiting for?" Pep continued to smile at her. In his hand he held a sign with the name *M. Van*.

That was surely his professional kindness, she told herself. She stammered something about a friend from Hamburg. Somehow, she couldn't get a clear sentence out. At the same time, her eyes wandered over the new throng of people streaming out of the gate. One man looked vaguely familiar, but she focused on the women, trying to spot Suzie.

At that moment, her mobile phone rang. The display showed a call from Jasmin. She smiled apologetically at Pep and pressed the green button.

"Hello, I'm just ..."

"Mum, just a minute, listen ..."

"Irene! How nice of you to pick me up!" Suddenly Suzie was standing next to her.

This time Irene had missed the fact that the gate doors had opened again.

Suzie was dragging a suitcase behind her and had a bag slung over her shoulder. In her hand she held a bag with the imprint of a bakery. Of course, she was well supplied with provisions.

"Jasmin, I'm at the airport, I can't talk right now."

She rang off without a greeting. In the crowd of people coming out of the gate, a familiar face caught her eye. A colleague of her husband? The name was on the tip of her tongue, but she couldn't think of it.

Suzie fell around her neck. No sooner had she let go of her friend than she turned to Pep. "I'm Suzie." Smiling, her friend held out her hand to Pep.

This did not suit Irene, even if she did not know why. "My advisor, Josep Folch i Bosch". She introduced him formally.

Pep nodded at Suzie, still with a smile on his lips. See, Irene scolded herself, that's his professional facial expression for female clients and girlfriends of his clients. Or he is a womaniser and smiles at every woman. Then she pushed the thought away and reached for Suzie's suitcase. She said goodbye to Pep as coolly as possible, then directed Suzie towards the car park where her car was parked.

"He looks gorgeous," Suzie remarked.

Of course, she could not let the sight of a male being go without comment. Irene grunted something vaguely. Suzie had a high attrition rate for men, but always complained about not being able to find an honest, faithful partner.

"Why do you have so much luggage?" she said.

Suzie's suitcase completely filled the boot of the small rental car. "You have to be prepared for everything," her friend said cheerfully, heaving her bag into the back seat. How had the monstrosity passed as hand luggage?

Irene suspected that Suzie had packed a complete evening wardrobe in addition to beach clothes. In case an admirer unexpectedly invited her to the opera or something. Then she suppressed her sarcastic thoughts. Basically, she was glad to have the friend by her side.

She curved through the multi-storey car park, left the airport grounds and threaded her way into the after-work traffic that flowed doggedly from Barcelona into the suburbs. It would take them a while to get to Cambrils.

CHAPTER TWENTY

IRENE PARKED in front of the flat. Later she could look for a better parking space, but for now the luggage had to be unloaded.

No sooner had she opened the boot than she heard a voice behind her: "Can I help you ladies?"

Carlos! The neighbour was omnipresent.

"You're welcome!" Suzie fluted.

Carlos heaved the suitcase out of the car, loaded the hand luggage onto his back and carried everything into the house. Before they knew it, Suzie's luggage was upstairs. "Can I buy you a drink as a little thank you?" said Suzie, flirting.

Irene rolled her eyes. She would have preferred to sit alone with Suzie on the balcony and watch the sun sink behind the mountains and kiss the sea with its last rays.

But Carlos happily accepted the invitation. Soon they had squeezed a third chair onto the balcony, were drinking cava with orange juice and talking trivia. Irene watched as her neighbour rose to the occasion. It was clear that he wanted to impress Suzie. The two of them didn't even know that they shared a passion for yoga. The question 'And what do you do?' had not yet come up.

Suzie brushed a strand of hair out of her face and looked up at

Carlos. She did it unconsciously, flirting at every opportunity and taking whatever came her way. Irene admired her easy-going lifestyle, but was repelled at the same time. Suzie always remained non-committal. At the same time, she longed for the great, the one love.

A love that Irene had thought she would live. But what good had it done her to stand faithfully by a man? She had been taken advantage of like a naïve teenager, or so it seemed. Irene thought about having another glass of champagne, but quickly dismissed the idea. On holiday she had once observed middle-aged women in hotels having a drink with breakfast and drinking their way through the day. She didn't want to end up like that.

Irene noticed that Suzie was looking at her. What was it about? She hadn't noticed how the conversation had developed.

"Are you coming to the beach?" Suzie repeated her question.

Irene hesitated. Actually, it wasn't a bad idea to stretch her legs again. She could understand that Suzie wanted to go to the sea right away. Then she saw the demanding look Carlos gave Suzie. Let the two of them go alone. Irene would sit on the balcony and look out at the sea until it was completely dark.

"You go on your own," she said.

Suzie protested, but it sounded half-hearted.

The two gathered their things, said goodbye, and set off.

Irene put her legs on the balcony railing and relaxed. After the stuffy air at the airport, she enjoyed the coolness of the evening.

She must have dozed off, because when she woke up again, the sun had already set. Goose bumps covered her arms as the warmth had also disappeared.

Irene went back into the flat. She noticed that the rubbish bin was overflowing. Suzie could have seen that, she thought angrily. Then she swallowed her displeasure and grabbed the bin bag. The short walk out of the door would get her circulation going again before she got ready for bed. There was no sign of Suzie or Carlos outside. She checked her mobile briefly, there were no new messages.

Irene put on a light jacket, carefully closed the door behind her and took the rubbish down. When she came back from the waste container and stepped into the hallway, she suddenly felt a movement behind her.

Before she could turn around, a strong arm wrapped around her throat from behind. Her windpipe was squeezed shut. Irene gasped. She tried to kick backwards, but the arm around her throat squeezed her air even harder.

Then she felt something cold on her neck.

"No bitching!"

CHAPTER TWENTY-ONE

IRENE'S HEART beat like crazy. She gasped frantically for air.

The pressure on her throat was eased a little. But the arm around her neck pulled her inexorably into the dark corner next to the back door, which could not be seen from the entrance.

"Where is my ring?" hissed a female voice.

Irene gave a muffled gurgle.

The woman continued to hold a knife to her throat.

"Don't move or I'll stab you, bitch! Now, out with it: where's the ring?"

"What ring?" Her voice trembled.

"Don't play dumb!"

Irene mustered all her courage, pulled her right leg up and stamped on the foot of the woman standing behind her with all her might.

The arm then let go of her and the pressure of the knife on her throat eased instantly. Irene wheeled around, only to see the attacker slump down as a man rammed his fist into the stomach of Hubert's lover. Carlos! He had arrived just in time. Now he wrestled the knife from the woman lying on the ground.

Then Suzie put her arms around Irene's neck. "Are you OK?" she breathed into her ear.

Mechanically, Irene released herself from the embrace. She did not answer the question. Nothing was OK.

"How lucky Carlos heard something," Suzie babbled on. "He thought a burglar had sneaked into the hallway. After all, you did have a break-in the other day."

"Broke in?" asked Carlos.

Irene rolled her eyes. She didn't like the fact that the whole world knew her flat had been searched. Too late, now word would get around.

Irene pointed at the woman. "What are we going to do with her?" she asked. "She's not a stranger! But for her to show up here..."

Carlos dragged the little woman up and pushed her in front of him, keeping her firmly in a police grip.

She kept her eyes downcast.

"Press charges?" the neighbour suggested. "Assault with a weapon. That adds up."

Irene's thoughts were racing. If she reported the woman, she would have to explain a lot. Why she hadn't gone to the police after her flat had been searched. And then it would be difficult to conceal the existence of the cash in the fridge. No, police were out of the question.

"Upstairs." She pointed in the direction of her flat.

Carlos pushed the woman in front of him up the stairs. The others followed. Fortunately, no one bumped into them. Irene was relieved when she closed her flat door behind her. Suzie immediately disappeared into the kitchen. Cupboard doors rattled. She was probably looking for sweets.

Carlos shoved the prisoner roughly onto the sofa. "Out with it! Who are you?"

Irene sat down in an armchair. She involuntarily grabbed her neck. She felt certain there were red strangulation marks there. She had only just escaped being strangled. Or was it just a threat? The scene played over and over again in her mind.

"That's my husband's mistress," Irene heard herself say. Her voice sounded strangely neutral.

Three pairs of eyes stared at her, all equally amazed.

"I am Madlen Wrobel," said the woman. "And I am Hubi's fiancée, not his mistress."

When she heard her husband's name come out of his lover's mouth, something broke inside Irene. Hubert had always refused to accept pet names. It sounds silly, he had said. And now this tramp was calling him 'Hubi'.

"He was my husband. He can't be engaged to you." Irene tried to keep a clear mind.

"He wanted a divorce." Madlen pulled her mobile phone out of her pocket and wiped the screen. Triumphantly, she held out the screen to Irene. It showed a photo of a hand with a diamond ring.

"The ring is mine. I left it here on my last visit," said Madlen. "You have to give it back. And the money too."

"What money?" asked Carlos.

CHAPTER TWENTY-TWO

"THE RING IS PROBABLY in the trash," Irene said, feeling a secret gloating. "I got rid of all the odds and ends in the drawers."

Madlen gasped.

"And the money is with the police," said Irene. "They searched the flat."

How easily the words escaped her lips. It felt safer to pretend the notes were no longer in her flat.

"They are investigating it. There are investigations in connection with Hubert's death." How awful that sounded. Dying. How stilted it sounded. He had been shot.

"What is there to investigate?" said Madlen, who sounded genuinely surprised. "I had planned to buy a new bikini. Hubi was going to leave two hundred euros on my kitchen table for that. Where's the money?"

"Two hundred euros?" Irene didn't know whether she should be relieved because Madlen obviously didn't know about the large amounts of cash still stored in the freezer. Or whether she should be horrified because the woman had such expensive tastes.

"You shouldn't have given the money to the police. Where did you get that idea?"

"Did he give you money for other things?"

"The studies, of course."

Now it was Irene's turn to gasp. "The studies?"

"Don't you trust me? I have enrolled for law. How am I supposed to pay for my studies now?"

Irene didn't care at all.

"Get a job, perhaps?"

She deliberately used a provocative undertone in her voice. She remembered how Hubert and she had spent every penny to pay their rent, in their first small flat together back then. This woman disrupted her whole life, held a knife to her neck and had the cheek to make demands. The architecture firm was doing well, but not so well that Hubert could finance a complete education for his mistress. After all, that cost at least a thousand dollars a month. A luxury bikini was nothing compared to that. Irene choked out: "Hubert didn't have that much money.

"Hubi has successfully invested in Bitcoins. 'Cryptocurrencies are the gold of the future', he used to say." Madlen puffed her chest out. "His profits were better than good."

Irene's heart lifted. At last there was a plausible explanation for Hubert's sudden wealth. Although she struggled to imagine him being so adventurous. He had never mentioned cryptocurrencies to her. It annoyed her that this bimbo seemed to know more about her husband than she did. The man she had shared a bed with night after night. Although, that wasn't true recently. She remembered all the nights she had lain alone in bed because Hubert had spent the night on the sofa in the living room - supposedly so as not to disturb her - or in some hotel on a business trip. On a supposed business trip, she corrected herself. He must have been in Madlen's arms, here in this flat in Cambrils. Anger boiled up inside her.

"What are you doing here, anyway," she demanded.

"I'm entitled to the flat. Hubi promised it to me when I got engaged. It was my present. He wanted to go to the notary and have me entered in the land register. But that never happened."

"Whatever he has promised, my daughter and I are the sole heirs of all his property; this flat included. Was it you who broke in here and searched everything?"

Madlen nodded weakly. "The ring ..." she stuttered.

"Silence!"

Irene could not bear to hear that Hubert had deceived her like this. Maybe this engagement ring actually existed. Well, until she had dumped the contents of the bedside cabinet in the rubbish. Then Irene remembered what the policeman had told her on the phone about a second person in the car.

"Were you there when Hubert died?"

Madlen began to sob. Between sobs, she gasped for breath.

The others looked at each other in concern.

"We're all very upset," said Suzie. "Something sweet would do us good. Calming food." She got up and went to the kitchen counter. "Do you have any ice cream?"

Without waiting for an answer, she opened the fridge.

"Stop! I don't have any!" Irene realised her voice sounded shrill. "Close the fridge again!"

"Okay."

Suzie gave her an irritated look and closed the fridge.

"There's a bar of chocolate in the drawer next to the sink." Irene managed to say, in an almost normal tone. She had visualised Suzie, looking for ice cream, pushing the packet of spinach aside and dislodging the money onto the kitchen floor. Madlen would have thrown herself at the notes and snatched them all.

Suzie rummaged around in the kitchen, came back to hand out chocolate chips to everyone, including Madlen. Then she stepped behind Irene's chair, bent over it, and began to massage her friend's shoulders. "You poor thing, you're still in shock," she murmured.

Carlos leaned over the sofa and put his arms on Madlen's shoulders from behind. He soothed her until her sobs subsided. Suzie gave Carlos a look that Irene could not interpret.

Madlen swallowed hard. "It was the worst day of my life."

CHAPTER TWENTY-THREE

"WE WENT TO HAMBURG," Madlen told her after she had calmed down a bit. "We had spent a week in Alsace, tasting wine and stuff."

Irene gasped. And she had once again fallen for the fairy tale about a conference.

Madlen paid no attention to her reaction. "We had almost reached Hamburg. We had only about another hour or two to go, depending on the traffic. We were late leaving because ..."

She glanced at Irene, then refrained from finishing the sentence.

"Anyway, we were late, after midnight. All of a sudden, out of nowhere, a car came from behind, and pulled into the lefthand lane. The car drove up alongside us and I heard a bang."

She sobbed again.

Irene surprised herself when she got up from the armchair and sat down next to Madlen on the sofa. She put her arm around her shoulder. She couldn't imagine what she would be going through if she herself had been sitting in the car with Hubert at that moment.

Madlen continued in a monotone voice: "Hubert slumped over and the car crashed into the crash barrier. There was this horrible screeching sound." Madlen doubled over and Irene stroked her back.

"Hubert ... Hubi's head had gone. There was nothing. Just blood and ..."

She swallowed hard. Everyone stared at her. She swallowed again and continued to speak, still in that impassive voice: "I was dazed, but then I realised that I was unharmed. Could move and everything. I threw myself out of the car and ran away in a panic."

Irene patted her. She struggled to block out the image of her husband sitting in the car without his head. Her chest tightened.

"There was a huge bang, and a fireball shot up into the sky behind me. I just kept stumbling away from there. I don't know where I was. I was out of my mind with fear. At some point I found myself at a bus stop, near some village. That's where I sat down. I just sat there and froze. It was so cold"

She bent over, cupped her face in her hands and sobbed.

Suzie touched Madlen on the shoulder and held out a tissue.

Madlen took it, blew her nose violently. Then she continued. "When it got light, a bus came and I got on it, just like that, without a ticket and everything. It stopped at some small town railway station, I don't know where. Then I went to Hamburg, which wasn't far."

Madlen looked up. "And that was it. Just like that. Like in a horror film."

"They shot at you from a car?"

Suzie seemed the least touched by the story, or at least she was the first to recover. Carlos' eyes simply widened and Irene tried to suppress the images that the story had evoked in her.

"Who was in the car?" Suzie persisted.

"I don't know, the windows were dark. Well, the passenger window was rolled down, I think. Otherwise, they couldn't have shot, could they?"

Madlen looked uncertainly around. "It happened very quickly, I didn't notice anything. I can't give any details about the car either. A family van or something, dark. Dark blue, grey or black. That's all I know."

"Did Hubert's car blow up?" Irene refused to acknowledge it as 'our car', but actually she had always seen it as the family car, even though it was Hubert's company car.

"I heard a huge explosion. But I didn't look around, I just kept running."

"A truck driver reportedly found him. He must have tried to extinguish the fire."

"Like I said, I don't know what happened after that." Madlen pulled the sleeves of her jumper over her hands. "I just ran away in a panic."

"Did you tell all this to the police?" asked Irene. She remembered the call from Inspector Kroeger, who had asked about the passenger.

"I don't want anything to do with them."

Madlen folded her arms in front of her chest.

"You have to make a statement. There is a witness who saw you. You should volunteer before the police come looking for you."

Irene took out her mobile phone. "I'll give you the number of the inspector in charge."

Before she could search the address book, the mobile phone rang. On the display was *Jasmin*.

Carlos rose. "I'm going home then."

He seemed to regret it. He would probably tell Araceli, Juan and all the neighbours what exciting things he had experienced, Irene thought. She pushed away her daughter's call. She would call back tomorrow after getting some sleep.

CHAPTER TWENTY-FOUR

FOSCA LAID her shaggy head trustingly on van Vreeden's lap. Pep suppressed a grin. He had recently walked along the beach with Fosca for an hour and the dog still had sand in her fur. Small threads of seaweed stuck to her hairy chin now clung to the Hamburg architect's suit trousers. Van Vreeden looked at her pleadingly, but apparently shied away from pushing the dog aside. Yet Fosca was as peaceful as she was tall. A soulful dog, and extremely intelligent.

Pep took pity on him.

"Fosca, vine!"

He took the biscuit from the saucer and held it out to the dog which immediately started drooling, some of the saliva again landing on van Vreeden's trouser leg. Then the dog came over to him and carefully accepted the biscuit.

Why was the architect wearing a fine suit? The German had insisted on meeting him immediately. Pep had already headed for the café on the promenade, after all it was Saturday. He would only enter his office for a very good reason, like an appointment with an attractive woman, but not with van Vreeden. Now the silver-haired man repeated his request for the third time, even though Pep had so far pointed out with elegant phrases that Irene Hansen was his client, and not VHB, Van Vreeden's company. If he was honest with himself, he had also arranged the meeting in the café because he hoped to run into her here by chance. Which had not been the case so far. Manfred van Vreeden did not let up.

"Can you tell me what business Daurada Ltda is set up for?"

"You can find all the necessary information in the commercial register. I will gladly send you the link."

"Just between us, what is the company involved in? Are there any construction projects planned?"

Pep smiled obligingly, even though the man was getting on his nerves. The Germans always got straight to the point and didn't understand that an evasive answer signified a no. He had to be clearer: "Unfortunately, I cannot give you any information that is not publicly available anyway. Daurada Ltda. has passed into the ownership of Irene Hansen and her daughter. They are the only persons to whom I am allowed to give information. Please understand that. I will be happy to help you with other matters."

He gave van Vreeden his usual business presentation, pointing out his bilingualism and illustrating the pitfalls of Spanish business life with examples. He also emphasised his boss Don Enrique's high standing and connections in Catalan society, which opened many doors.

"It may well be that our office VHB needs your services," said van Vreeden.

It was a lure, Pep understood. He took a sip of the excellent coffee and peered along the promenade, but couldn't catch sight of Irene's petite figure. She was probably sleeping late on the weekend.

The estate agent his Gestoria worked with strolled past, speaking into his mobile phone through a headset. He nodded to Pep, raised his hand in greeting and turned towards the entrance of the apartment complex where Irene's flat was located.

"Can you help me with something?" asked van Vreeden at that moment.

Pep had not been listening and had to ask. "What are we talking about?"

"The hotel in Salou. How involved was Hubert Hansen there?"

Pep's brain was rattling. He had taken over the management for

Hansen's letterbox company when a colleague left. In all those years, the client had not come forward, he had never met him personally. And the Daurada Ltda. was merely a construct to purchase the holiday flat in a tax-efficient way. Which now benefited the heirs, as no inheritance tax was due. He had never heard of a hotel in Salou in connection with Hansen. He told Manfred van Vreeden that.

The man from Hamburg took in this new information. He sipped his coffee thoughtfully. Latte, of course. 'Americano' was what the waiters disparagingly called the drink. The Germans did not appreciate the taste of pure, strong espresso.

Finally, van Vreeden said: "My partner was responsible for the construction of a hotel complex in Salou. I would like to know what the status of the work is. Unfortunately, I can't access his computer at the moment. Can you help me with that?"

Pep pondered. If the architect had died in the middle of a building project, who could step in? Surely the Hamburg office was the most likely. "If you give me the address of the hotel, I can find out how far the project has progressed," he finally promised. One had to keep these clients warm, perhaps they would continue to be involved in Catalonia and needed the Gestoria's support. Don Enrique would pay him a bonus if he acquired a new German client. Manfred van Vreeden seemed dissatisfied with his information, but eventually relaxed.

Fosca seemed to sense that the conversation was coming to an end. The dog was far too intelligent. The Catalan dog breed had been bred to herd sheep and understand every word the shepherd said. Life as a family dog was underwhelming for Fosca, especially since neither Montse nor Pep had children to romp around with. Now she jumped up and shook herself enterprisingly, splashing mud and dirt on van Vreeden's trouser leg.

CHAPTER TWENTY-FIVE

AT THE DOOR of the flat stood a man in a suit, his hair slicked back and carefully shaved. A slim leather briefcase was stuck under his arm.

"Good morning, my name is Sanchez, from Immobilaria Costa Daurada," said the one with the gel hairdo.

He spoke clear, correct German with a slight accent. He held out his hand to Irene and smiled at her.

"Yes, come in." Irene had completely forgotten about the estate agent. She offered him coffee, but he waved her off.

He looked out of the window at the sea, which was shimmering dark blue today. "Nice view! Very good location, your flat."

His gaze roamed around the room, taking in the kitchenette and the balcony, which seemed tiny to Irene at that moment. "Do you have a floor plan?"

If there was one at all, it was in Hamburg, Irene thought. She shook her head.

"Then I will measure the flat so that our software can create a floor plan. We need that for the advertisement on the internet."

He pulled out a device that projected laser dots onto the wall. He pressed buttons on the device and muttered to himself. Finally, he looked up. "The balcony only covers half a square metre, but you probably know that."

Irene nodded mechanically. Small, but mine, she thought. The mornings on the balcony, the view of the sea, that was priceless. She thought with horror of the dull, grey days in Hamburg.

"May I have a look at the Master Bedroom?" the estate agent asked.

Irene knew it was a rhetorical question, but she would have preferred to answer in the negative and throw the idiot out. But she pointed towards the bedroom door. Didn't have the strength to go with him.

When the man had disappeared into the bedroom, she went to the kitchen counter. She filled the coffee maker with agitated hands. Even if the estate agent didn't want any, she desperately needed caffeine. The discussion with Madlen had dragged on late into the night.

There was a knock at the door. She opened it and let Suzie in. "Where is Madlen?" she hissed at her. She had slept on the sofa, and Suzie had slept next to Irene in the marital bed. Even before Irene had risen, Suzie had shown the slut out.

"She'll never show her face here again if she's smart. She's on her way to Barcelona and is taking the next flight to Hamburg. Or did you want to report her?"

"No way," Irene whispered. She definitely didn't want to have any more to do with the police than was absolutely necessary. At least not until she knew where the cash in the freezer had come from. She just needed peace and quiet to figure out the next steps. To find out what Hubert had really been up to.

The estate agent came back into the living space. "Well, it's fifty-seven square metres in total. The balcony with the sea view is an important extra. I estimate the flat at ..."

He paused for effect. His gaze went to Suzie, who smiled at him. She flirted with every man, thought Irene. Yet this Sanchez is half our age. Besides, he was a slimy guy.

The broker gave Suzie a professionally charming smile, turned back to Irene. He mentioned the sum of four hundred thousand euros, which made her gasp. She had not expected that. The amount would be enough to completely renovate her hotel. But would she exchange this flat for mere euros? Did the money replace the view of the sea? She heard herself asking for more.

"But of course we will put a higher price in the ad," Sanchez replied. "Then we have room for negotiation."

"I am serious about this. The price must be higher."

The guy looked at her as if she was mentally retarded. "We work with a platform that uses artificial intelligence. Our valuation software knows all the transactions in the region over the last few years. It has determined a sum that is marketable. If the price in the ad is set higher, it takes longer to market."

It would take longer, so what? She caught herself thinking that maybe she could come back later in the spring, if the hotel business allowed it.

The broker looked at her like a teacher at an obtuse pupil. He said something about 'ineffective', praised his software again and called her 'madam'. She hadn't heard that expression for a while. When she continued to hesitate, he relented, "We can put a higher price in the ad, no problem." He took a form out of his briefcase, filled in a few fields and placed the paper on the dining table with a grand gesture." We will follow your instructions. If you'll sign here, please."

He pointed to a dotted line at the foot of the leaf.

Everything in her rebelled against signing the contract. But she took the pen the estate agent held out to her and put her name under the text. "At this price, it will take longer to market," he warned again.

Her phone rang and when she saw Pep's name on the display, she took the call while waving the estate agent away towards the door and calling after him another 'Gracias y buenos días'.

CHAPTER TWENTY-SIX

Pep stood at the door of the office and beamed at her.

Sea-blue eyes, no doubt about it, Irene thought. Involuntarily she beamed back.

He led her into his office and she sank into the leather chair in front of his desk.

"I'm sorry to bother you at the weekend, but there are still some forms to sign. First of all, do you want to change the account here in Spain to your name and keep it? The utilities for the flat, like electricity and water, come out of that."

Irene's eyes snapped open. She had not the slightest desire to deal with bureaucratic matters. She hadn't known about an account in Spain. Of course not, you stupid chicken, she scolded herself. She was clueless. Account, flat, cash, mistress ... Hubert could hardly have debited incidental expenses for a flat in Spain from their joint account in Hamburg, she would have noticed. Besides, even in the age of SEPA, it was certainly easier to keep a local account. She sighed and bent over the papers Pep held out to her.

He explained the individual steps he recommended to her and obligingly answered her questions.

He doesn't want anything from you, that's purely professional kindness, Irene inculcated herself. She tried not to stare at him. Apart from his blue eyes, he also had a well-toned figure. No wonder, if he was out on the beach every morning with that shaggy of a dog.

When the whole stack of papers had been worked through, Irene remembered what Madlen had told her. "Did my husband own Bitcoin?" she asked off the top of her head.

"Bitcoin?" Pep raised his eyebrows in amazement. "That internet currency? Not that I know of. The records don't show anything." He hesitated for a moment, then said, "I'm not familiar with it. But as I said, there's no mention of Bitcoins in the papers."

A man who admitted that he had no idea about anything. That was rare. Irene scored a point for Pep in her mind. Then she admonished herself not to do that. No one had to score here. Irene forced herself to think of something else. The upcoming weekend, for example. She could do something with Suzie, show her the area. But she didn't know the area herself yet, apart from the beach she had walked along every morning.

"Do you miss Hamburg?" asked Pep at that moment, as if he had guessed her thoughts.

She blinked at him in confusion. "No, I ..."

She broke off. Started again. "I like living there, even if the weather is mixed. But there are beautiful sides. Now, for example, the apple blossom will soon begin." She thought of trips to the Old Country. "The trees are blossoming snow-white, with a slight touch of pink." What was she talking about? What did Pep care about fruit blossom. Surely he had only inquired about her homeland out of politeness.

"Tomorrow is Sunday, even Gestors don't have to work. Do you have any plans?" asked Pep. He continued talking quickly, as if he wanted to forestall a negative answer. "There are hardly any apple trees growing here, but the almond blossom has started. We could drive into the hinterland and I'll show you the beauty of the almond groves."

Irene nodded. That would be a wonderful plan. Explore the hinterland with Pep at her side. Then she chided herself. What kind of woman was she? She had just buried her husband, now she was going off with someone else? Yet her husband had cheated on her for years, did she owe him fidelity? Beyond death? Then she remembered Suzie. "My friend is visiting. I don't want to leave her alone."

"She can come with us after all," said Pep. Did that sound regretful?

Irene nodded. "I'll ask her and get back to you."

They said goodbye. On the way to the door, they passed Pep's boss's office; its door was open. Don Enrique was talking to a tall, silver-haired man. The visitor turned around. At that moment she recognised him.

Manfred van Vreeden.

Automatically, Irene nodded at him. She had seen him the other day. Fleetingly, out of the corner of her eye. In Hamburg? No, at the airport in Barcelona! He had come out of the gate with a swarm of people when she had picked up Suzie.

Then she remembered the sign Pep had held up. *M. Van.* Not an Asian Mister Van, but Manfred van Vreeden. Perhaps one of the Spaniards had mistaken the 'van' for the first of two surnames, as was common in this country. What was her husband's partner doing here? And in the Gestoria, of all places? This wasn't a holiday trip after all.

She bit her lips. Tomorrow, when she took Pep - and Suzie, she reminded herself - on a trip to some almond trees, she would casually ask him about van Vreeden.

She said goodbye to Pep and imagined that he was looking deep into her eyes. A sea-blue radiance that touched her.

In her flat, Suzie sat on the balcony with a drink and looked out over the sea, which glistened in the light of the afternoon sun. "Beautiful, I would never go back to Hamburg if I were you." She raised a glass of an orange-red liquid, surely an Aperol Spritz, one of her favourite drinks. In front of her was a bowl of nuts.

Irene only mouthed off. Her hotel, which had taken her years to build, was waiting for her in Hamburg. It needed some renovations for which she had not had the money before. But now things looked different. Thinking about the hotel, she remembered that she had to call Jasmin back.

CHAPTER TWENTY-SEVEN

IRENE SAT DOWN WITH SUZIE. Eyed their apricot-coloured drink.

"Do you want to?" Suzie made an effort to get up.

Irene held her back, rose and fetched a glass and a bottle of red wine from the kitchen. Then she settled down for good next to Suzie, put her feet up on the balcony parapet and looked out to sea.

The sun conjured up sparks of light on the spray of the waves. Irene could not get enough of the spectacle. The red wine put her in a relaxed, somewhat enraptured mood.

They chatted about trivia. Only when the sun was already low did she overcome herself and ask Suzie if she would come with her tomorrow to see the almond blossom.

"I forgot to tell you. Carlos invited me." Suzie sipped her drink and looked at her over the rim of the glass uncertainly. "I hope you don't mind. After all, I came all this way so we could see each other." Again she took a sip of her drink. When Irene didn't respond, she said, "Carlos knows a secluded cove, he says no one goes there. Did you know he does yoga too?"

However, Irene knew that. For her part, was Suzie aware that Carlos preferred naked yoga? Irene pushed aside the image of the unclothed, contorted male body on the neighbouring balcony. In front of that came the image of her friend squatting in a yoga seat on a lonely beach with Carlos, both of them without clothes, of course. She herself would sink into the ground with shame if an innocent walker came around the corner and saw her in such a situation.

Then she realised what Suzie's plan meant and her heart did a little hop. She would be travelling alone with Pep without a care in the world. Neither did she have to feel guilty about leaving her friend behind alone, nor would Suzie disturb their togetherness. Then she chased the thought away. Pep wanted to do his client a favour, that was all. Perhaps he was already regretting his offer to show her around. "We can do something together next week."

Suzie nodded. "How are you doing with all this, anyway?" The friend made a vague, sweeping motion with her arm.

Irene took a big sip of wine. How was she? She had avoided thinking about it.

"If there's anything I can do for you ...", Suzie put in.

"You knew all along?" Irene looked her straight in the eye.

"about Madlen?" Suzie narrowed her eyes. "I always thought you knew. Would tolerate it. You hardly saw each other anyway."

"The hotel ..."

"Oh, dear, the hotel, isn't that an excuse? It works even if you're not there for a day. And now Jasmin can..."

"Jasmin is still far too young for this responsibility. If none of us stop by, how fast do you think the mice dance on the table? The staff changes all the time, it's crazy hard to even find someone for room service. I can't pay the salaries like an Atlantic or Sheraton."

"How old were you when you took over the hotel? No older than Jasmin either. You have to let go."

Irene thought she had to call her daughter back. She took another sip of wine, surprised to notice that the glass was empty. "That was a completely different situation. I was young, okay, but there was no alternative then."

"You could have found employment."

Irene thought back. Suzie was right. But a chance to take over her own house would not have presented itself again so soon. Even if the building had been pretty run-down at the time. She had realised the full extent of the renovations too late. By then she could no longer withdraw from the purchase contract. She had thrown herself into work without looking back. There had been little time for romantic evenings with Hubert. She always thought that he had been understanding, because he himself had been working overtime after overtime. Overtime. She gasped. If there really had been any. She hoped that at least back then, in the early days of their marriage, he had remained faithful to her. In front of Suzie and everyone else, she had always maintained the façade of a happy relationship. In front of herself, too. She had never admitted to herself that anything was wrong. Obviously, a lot had gone wrong.

She refilled her glass. The red wine was heavy and velvety on her tongue. The alcohol made her dizzy, but it also made her feel snivelling. She pulled herself together. At least until Jasmin was born, her marriage had been happy, she told herself. After that, life had become even more stressful, she rotated between the baby and the hotel. Hubert had withdrawn more and more from caring for the child. At that time, he had started sleeping in the office for a night now and then.

She remembered how Jasmin had gone through the childhood illnesses. Her daughter had been prone to colds and flu. Many a night she had sat by the bedside of the feverish child, murmuring soothing words, changing calf compresses - while Hubert had entrenched himself behind files piled up on the kitchen table. After the move, he had then had his study. While she calculated the monthly balance sheets of the hotel at the kitchen table.

Should she have taken more time for Hubert? Let business be business for a change? Was it her own fault that her marriage was apparently built on sand? She finished her glass in one gulp and poured another.

"I was such an ass!"

"Nonsense! You're a kind-hearted person and you can't imagine anyone betraying you."

Suzie clearly had a glorified image of her. Irene saw herself more as a naïve little mouse. Perhaps she also lacked any female instinct. Shouldn't she have realised that she had lost Hubert's love?

"He would have divorced me. I didn't suspect anything." She took another sip of wine. The alcohol put a merciful veil over her pain.

"We don't know," Suzie said dryly. She nibbled some nuts in front of her. "Only Madlen claims that. Maybe Hubert was stringing her along and didn't want to part with you at all."

"But the ring ..."

"The ring could be from the flea market. Do we know if she really got it from Hubert? I don't trust her. She can claim anything now."

Irene nodded to herself. It would be nice if Suzie was right. She wanted to believe in it firmly.

"Hubert always kept me short. There is no money for big jumps. Representation was important, hence the big company car, his watch ... and he gives this tramp a ring and gives her two hundred euros for a bikini."

Irene swallowed. Her own swimming costume had cost less than fifty euros in a sale. Well, you knew ... the less fabric, the more expensive the swimwear.

Suzie put her arm around her: "Maybe that was on purpose. He wanted a sweet little mouse to play the big man to. To compensate for the strong woman at his side. He adored you, I'm sure of it. It wasn't serious with Madlen."

CHAPTER TWENTY-EIGHT

PEP GREETED Irene with four kisses, alternately right and left on each cheek.

Irene held her breath so as not to expel any alcohol breath. This morning she had found two empty bottles of red wine in the kitchen without remembering that they had opened and drunk the second one. Suzie had stuck to the Aperol, hadn't she?

The shaggy dog jumped up at her until Pep reprimanded him. He looked offended.

They got into Pep's little white Seat.

The dog made itself at home in the back seat.

The light of the sun was painfully blinding. She put on a pair of sunglasses. The two aspirin this morning had dulled the headache a little.

"How about breakfast in a medieval town?" Pep accelerated briskly, causing Irene's stomach to clench. She tried to smile politely and nodded.

As always, Pep was dressed chic but casual. He looked attractive in a cool way, his blue eyes sparkling. She wondered why he had invited her. Probably out of pity.

"Beautiful weather," he remarked.

She hummed in agreement. Had no idea what she could contribute to the small talk.

Pep seemed to understand that she was not yet ready to talk. He drove briskly. It was a dual carriageway, first through flat land, then the road narrowed and wound over a pass. When Pep parked, Irene realised she had dozed off.

"A café con leche?"

Irene nodded. They passed through a medieval town wall with towers and battlements. The little town looked lost in time - it seemed unchanged for centuries.

Pep told us something about the history of the small town. Supposedly, it was the home of Saint George, who was called Sant Jordi here.

Irene noticed that many shops had placed a dragon in the shop window, as a figure on a poster, made of wood as a child's toy or just as decoration.

The dog took the opportunity to pee at every corner.

Pep led them to a square overshadowed by plane trees. In one of the cafés they had a hearty breakfast: orange juice, croissants and a pastry dusted with icing sugar, so-called ensaimadas. The strong coffee finally awakened Irene's spirits.

She remembered that she had wanted to call her daughter for days. She excused herself and dialled Jasmin's number.

"Mum?" The daughter's voice sounded occupied.

"Hello, my dear. I couldn't take your call, you wouldn't believe what's going on." Irene reflected that she had even pushed away Jasmin's calls twice, if she remembered correctly.

"I'm still in bed, Leon is here."

Leon, who was Leon? She suppressed the question just in time. Back in Hamburg, she would find out who this Leon was and what he meant in Jasmin's life.

A sparrow landed at Irene's feet and pecked at the crumbs that had fallen. Then he looked at her demandingly. He ignored the huge dog. Irene had to smile.

"When are you coming back?" asked Jasmin.

Irene thought about it. She hadn't booked a return flight yet and hadn't given it a thought. Events had been coming thick and fast lately. "I don't know exactly."

"Mum, we need to discuss how to proceed with the hotel. Now that there is enough money. I have ..."

The waitress came and asked for her wishes. Irene pointed to her coffee cup. Into her mobile phone she said, "Let's talk when I get back, I have some things to do here."

Jasmin sighed and wished them a good day.

When she had finished talking, Irene congratulated herself on not asking who Leon was. It was unusual for her daughter to still be in bed on Saturday morning. Otherwise she was an early riser.

Pep put a hand on her arm. A warm, strong hand.

She looked up.

His sea-blue eyes sparkled. "Let Alemania rest and enjoy the day. I'll show you the almond blossom now."

The following hours flew by. Pep drove with her along tiny country roads to remote villages that seemed to be stuck to rocks. Olive and almond trees grew on terraces bordered by dry stone walls. Olive trees with mighty trunks that must have been hundreds of years old. In between, almond trees with gnarled branches.

Finally they parked at the edge of a country lane and walked through a white sea of blossoms. Bees buzzed back and forth between the branches. Again and again Irene stopped to take in the scent of one of the blossoms. She was happy.

At some point Pep put his arm around her waist.

She let it happen. After a while, she leaned lightly against his warm, strong body. There was nothing to it. Two people enjoying an outing.

The dog jumped happily around her.

After the hike through the almond groves, they drove on winding roads through small villages, tasted wine in a cellar - but Pep only sipped. Then they finally stopped in a tiny bar, where they enjoyed a menu that was as down-to-earth as it was tasty. It was accompanied by an earthy, full-bodied red. Irene had already forgotten that she had drunk too much yesterday and let herself enjoy the garnet-coloured grape juice. She wiped her mouth with the napkin and sighed happily.

Pep was satisfied that she liked it. When they drove back, they were silent, but it was not an uncomfortable silence, but the relaxed end of a nice day. It only became difficult when they said goodbye.

Irene would have liked to hug Pep, out of gratitude for the beautiful day. But did that give the wrong impression? After all, she didn't want anything from him. She was still grieving for Hubert, she told herself.

At that moment Pep broke the silence: "Are you free on Tuesday evening? How about we go to the fishermen's association restaurant? It's out on the pier and has brilliant fish." He looked at her.

Irene admired his deep blue eyes, not for the first time. The wrinkles around the rim deepened as he smiled now.

"You're welcome! And thank you for a great day." She straightened up on the tips of her feet and pressed a quick kiss to his cheek. That was just the way things were done around here. That couldn't be a wrong signal. Then she wuzzed the dog over the head, turned quickly and left. She was after all a Hanseatic woman who did not like to show her feelings in public.

As she unlocked the gate to the apartment complex, it struck her that she had not thought about Hubert for a single moment. Was she so unfaithful as to forget him shortly after his death? She suppressed the guilty conscience.

In the stairwell she bumped into Suzie, who was carrying several bags. When she saw Irene, she set them down and fell around her neck. Then she held them from her with outstretched arms. "You look good! Got some colour."

Irene noticed that the skin on her nose was burning. The pale skin was not used to the sun at this time of year.

"How was your day? We discovered a beautiful bay." Without waiting for Irene's answer, Suzie told her about yoga exercises together and a subsequent meditation on a rocky plateau right by the sea.

"He also has a really great pair of yoga pants, we went shopping right away and I got myself a pair of those too. There are really cute boutiques here and ..."

"He was wearing pants?"

"What else? A skirt maybe?" Suzie looked at her in irritation.

"You weren't naked?"

Suzie gasped. "What makes you think that?"

Irene told how she had seen Carlos on the balcony. "But don't tell him about it, he doesn't know I saw him."

"I'm silent as the grave." Suzie put her index finger to her mouth. But her eyes were glittering.

Irene helped Suzie carry the bags upstairs. At the top she sucked in her breath sharply.

The door of the flat hung crookedly on its hinges. The door frame was splintered in places. Someone had forced their way in.

"What happened here?" Irene's voice sounded sharp and high-pitched. The situation felt like déjà vu to her. For the second time in a few days, there had been a break-in. Had Madlen not returned to Hamburg after all? Was she still searching for the alleged engagement ring?

CHAPTER TWENTY-NINE

IN RESPONSE TO HIS GREETING, Montse only grunted at him. She blinked and handed him the leash. His sister had never been a morning person.

Fosca, on the other hand, was full of eagerness. She tugged at his trouser leg. As often as he looked after the dog, he might as well take her all to himself instead of always going past Montse. When they reached the beach, the dog raced ahead a few hundred yards, turned gracefully and ran back to Pep. His ears flapped in the wind.

Pep was immediately in a good mood. The nice weekend had also contributed to this. He had seen Irene every day and would have dinner with her tomorrow evening. His ploy had worked to lure her to the office on Saturday with the excuse of urgently needing to sign papers. Without hesitation, she had also agreed to his proposal for the outing. And it had been beautiful. Perhaps a German woman suited him better than a Catalan? Were his German roots so strong that there were automatic similarities? Maybe Ana was right when she accused him of square-jawedness, nit-picking and all the other German vices. Qualities that Irene would find positive?

In a good mood he picked up a piece of wood, it might once have been a table leg before the waves had ground it round. "Fosca!" With a lunging motion, he threw the stick in the direction of the waves.

The dog ran after it and with a few jumps had reached his destination. He purposefully grabbed the wood that Pep had thrown from all the flotsam, ran back to his master and circled him. It looked as if the animal was grinning.

Pep did not let himself be provoked into wanting to snatch the stick from her. He bent down for another stick, found a suitable one and threw it.

Fosca forgot the chair leg and jumped to fetch the new stick.

Pep thought again of the scene in the Gestoria. Irene had been amazed at the existence of a Spanish account. Was she a spoilt mistress, kept away from all business matters by her husband? That couldn't be, after all she ran her own hotel, if he had understood correctly. Had her husband kept secrets from her? If so, he had been a fool to betray such a sympathetic woman.

For which he himself had even broken his sacred principle of not working at the weekend. Just to see Irene. A day without meeting her seemed a gloomy day.

Then he remembered van Vreeden. He hadn't let him brush him off, but had marched straight to Don Enrique. Had he raved too much about his connections in elite Catalan circles? Had he overdone it with the acquisition? On the other hand, a respected Hamburg architect would be a good client and Don Enrique would praise him for having made the contact.

Fosca nudged him encouragingly. She was right, you should enjoy the day and not think too much about business.

It was still fresh on the beach, the first rays of sunshine did not have enough power to warm. He set off at a trot and jogged the last bit back. Fosca was thrilled and ran beside him with her tongue hanging out.

When he brought Fosca back to Montse's flat, she was sitting at the kitchen table drinking a coffee. The caffeine had provided her with enough energy that she could now greet Pep properly.

"Looking good, brother dear!" She looked at him more closely. "Are you too much in love?"

"What makes you think that?"

"That inner glow! The last time you had that was when you were dating Ana. I guess you'll have to get rid of her quickly." She grinned diabolically.

His stomach clenched. Montse was right, a discussion with Ana was overdue.

CHAPTER THIRTY

IRENE'S GAZE wandered over the objects scattered on the floor. The few books torn from the shelf, pots without lids next to the remains of her travel bag, which had been slit open several times. There were also large gaps in the upholstery of the sofa and the two armchairs. This time Madlen had taken a radical approach. But did it make sense? Was she looking for her engagement ring in the upholstery of the couch?

Suzie glanced over Irene's shoulders, sucked in a quick breath and slapped her hands over her mouth.

Irene hurried her to the fridge, opened it and tore open the freezer compartment. There, quietly and peacefully, lay the spinach packet. She reached in and felt for the banknotes. Immediately felt the pile of money. Whoever had searched the flat had not discovered it. Probably many people had had a traumatic encounter with spinach in their childhood and gave the packet a wide berth forever and ever. That's why the hiding place was so safe, she thought, and at the same moment wondered why she was thinking such petty thoughts in the face of the chaos.

Suzie had watched her action in wonder. "What are you looking for? Do you want an ice cream to calm you down? Or chocolate?" Without waiting for an answer, she began to rummage in her handbag. "Hang on, I think I have another chocolate bar."

"You always with your chocolate."

"Chocolate helps with everything." Suzie conjured two crushed bars from her pocket, tore off the plastic wrapper, looked at the contents with disgust, but then popped them in her mouth and chewed on them. She handed the other one to Irene. Suzie's gaze slid over the devastation in the room. "You obviously have enemies. Who on earth would do such a thing? This doesn't look like Madlen's work."

The same thought hammered behind Irene's forehead. "Who knew we weren't here today?"

"You don't think it was someone we know, do you? Maybe it's just a series of burglaries in holiday flats."

Irene didn't let herself be put off. "First, Carlos knew, second, Pep knew, third, everyone they told about their rendezvous." As she spoke, Irene held up first one, then two, then three fingers. "So probably half the town."

"Carlos didn't know you were out too. And Pep didn't know I was going out with Carlos."

"I told him about it. At least I think I did." Strained, Irene tried to remember when she had done that. Already before their trip or only on the way? Did Pep have a helper? Someone he just had to call or text to tell him it was a free-for-all? But what reason would the consultant have for searching her flat?

"Pep doesn't know about the money, but Carlos does. He was here when we talked about it."

"You took the money to the bank. There's no point in looking for it here."

"So whoever did this doesn't know about the safe deposit box," Irene concluded. "Carlos is already ruled out." That left Pep, if the perpetrator came from her small circle of acquaintances. Irene did not like the idea.

"I don't feel safe here. It scares me. Someone was very angry." Suzie pointed to the slashed sofa, the tattered cushions with their insides hanging out. "Glad I'm leaving tomorrow. You should come with me. It's too dangerous here."

She gasped.

"Why don't you try to book another ticket quickly? Pep is taking care of everything here until the agent sells the flat."

A stab went through Irene's heart. She should leave the flat to someone else? At the same time, she felt relieved that Suzie obviously trusted Pep. She didn't like to imagine that he was in cahoots with criminals. "I have a lot of paperwork to do."

"You can do all that online these days, can't you?"

Irene did not answer. Tomorrow evening she had an appointment with Pep at the restaurant in the harbour. Her heart fluttered when she thought about it. There was no way she would cancel and fly to Germany.

She stepped up to the kitchen counter. Fortunately, the bottles had only been moved and not destroyed. The damage was concentrated in places where something - money, for example - could be hidden. It wasn't wanton destruction, but a targeted search, Irene realised. She reached for the sherry bottle, took two water glasses and poured courageously, handing one to Suzie.

Silently they sipped the sweet, comforting liquid.

Then Irene was seized with rage. She began to tidy up frantically. Thundered the few books back onto the shelf, pushed back the wool from the slit cushions as best she could, draped them on the sofa so that the large slit in the cushion was no longer visible.

"Do you want to take pictures? For the insurance?"

Irene was not sure if this was an insurance case. Would the household insurance cover it? Had Hubert even taken out such a policy?

"Or call the police?"

That would probably be the most sensible thing to do. But how could Irene explain what had happened here without mentioning the money? My husband was a criminal, his enemies seem to hate him beyond death? Didn't really sound good.

Without answering, she picked up a few pens lying on the floor. Lost in thought, she opened the drawer of the sideboard where the TV was.

When she put the pens in, she saw a box with the logo of an electronics company. She took it out and opened it. Inside was a brand new mobile phone, albeit an old-fashioned clunky model with physical buttons, and the accompanying charger with cable. There were also three cardboard carriers for SIM cards in a bulge in the box, two were still shrink-wrapped. The third holder had been opened and the SIM card had been broken out. One mobile phone and three SIM cards?

"What have you got there?" Suzie looked curiously over her shoulder.

"I don't know." Irene pressed the power button on the phone, which came to life after some hesitation. The battery indicator was at half-full. The device asked for a PIN code to be entered.

She thought about it. Hubert had used his date of birth as the code for his iPhone - of course he had always bought the latest model, claiming that it was tax-deductible. She typed in his data. With a *pling!* the mobile phone opened.

"Wow, you're a real hacker," Suzie said.

The mobile phone didn't offer many possibilities, it could make phone calls and use SMS, as Irene found out. The tiny screen did not show any apps. She clicked through the items in the menu, which was green on a dark background. The language was set to Spanish, but she quickly found the list of calls. There were no outgoing calls at all, no text messages, only three calls had come in. It was always the same number, beginning with 0034, so here it was from Spain.

Irene directed the flashing cursor to the number and let her finger hover over the green button for 'call'.

CHAPTER THIRTY-ONE

"Don't do it!" said Suzie.

At that moment, Irene had already pressed. The call was building up. Irene selected the 'loudspeaker' function and they heard the ringing tone. Once, twice, three times.

"There's no answer," Suzie said.

At that moment, a man's voice spoke up. "Hola!"

"Hola!", Irene replied automatically.

There was a pause. Then the man said in Spanish, "You have something that belongs to us."

"What? Why?"

"You know exactly what I mean."

"I ..."

"Keep this phone, we'll contact you."

Then the connection was terminated.

Irene and Suzie looked at each other, perplexed.

"Who was that?"

"I don't know. Some guy." Irene put the phone back in the drawer, carefully, as if it were a loaded gun.

"What did he say?"

Irene translated the few words they had exchanged.

"I didn't understand anything, but it sounded threatening. And what a voice! Smooth as an eel."

Irene had concentrated on the words, not the voice. In retrospect, it seemed to her that the man on the other end of the line had complaints with his vocal cords. He had sounded hoarse. "He spoke in a singsong. Not like the people here." She thought about where she had heard this Spanish before. In the Peruvian restaurant in Hamburg?

"Like the people from South America."

"A Latino?"

Irene nodded.

"You should really come to Germany with me. Leave this matter to the police!"

Irene said nothing.

"This is far too dangerous!"

Irene thought about dinner at the 'Confraria del Port' restaurant tomorrow night with Pep. Should she give it a miss? No, said her heart. Flee to Hamburg!, said her mind.

Suddenly she was overcome by a tremendous rage. Why had Hubert left her alone? What had he done that she had to deal with a dangerous inheritance? Why was she now faced with such difficult decisions? Why couldn't she grieve in peace? She thundered the drawers shut with gusto.

"Let's sleep on it first." As long as Suzie was by her side, Irene didn't feel at risk. Suzie knew her way around every situation and never let it get her down. She still remembered exactly the day at vocational school when Suzie - then still Susanne - had been late, had a run in her tights and had breathlessly sat down in the empty seat next to Irene. Since then they had been inseparable. But working in the hotel business had become too exhausting for Susanne. She quit, took a trip to Goa - it was supposed to be a world trip, but she ran out of money on the way - and when she came back, she demanded that everyone call her only Suzie. And no, not Susi, but Suzie with a Z. On Goa she had got to know yoga. Fascinated, she attended one class after another, became a trainer herself and opened her own studio as soon as she had saved enough. After a few years, she had moved from a backyard in Eimsbüttel to a popular location in this Hamburg district. Suzie knew an incredible number of people and managed to get them interested in yoga. Even Irene had struggled onto the mat a few times, but then the hotel had taken up all her time again.

"When I'm back in Hamburg, I'll sign up for one of your courses."

"Now how do you figure that?"

"Need to move more. The back, you know."

"It can also be psychological. All the stress. Yoga will help you get back into balance. Yesterday on the beach with Carlos, that was incredible. The air, the smell of the sea, the calls of the birds ... just perfect." Suzie smiled happily.

Irene envied her. Her friend could simply let herself go. She lived in the here and now while she herself was always brooding. In any case, she was glad that she had dissuaded Suzie from the subject of going home. She said with more alacrity than she really felt, "I'll sort things out here and then come home. The hotel needs me."

She remembered that she hadn't spoken to Jasmin again. She would make up for it tomorrow, when Suzie had left. I wonder if there was trouble at the hotel because Jasmin had been trying to reach her all the time. But if there was trouble, she would have spoken of it yesterday, whether any Leon was beside her or not. At least Irene hoped so.

Suzie opened her suitcase, took out a bar of chocolate and offered Irene a piece.

Then she stuffed her clothes, which had somehow spread over the sofa, into the suitcase in a tangled ball. "There, I'll pack the rest in the morning. What are we going to do now?"

She looked at Irene, who was licking the chocolate off her fingers. "I have half a day left in this holiday paradise."

CHAPTER THIRTY-TWO

"WE COULD GO EAT fish on the promenade." Irene didn't feel half as adventurous as her friend, but on the other hand she should take the opportunity to go out to eat again. Sitting alone in a restaurant she found dreadful. If she went out with Suzie today and with Pep tomorrow, she would have to cook for herself on Wednesday at the earliest. Cooking for one person, she hadn't done that in decades. She decided to enjoy the time with Suzie and only take care of all business again tomorrow, after she left.

At that moment, her mobile phone rang. A Hamburg number. She licked the last bit of chocolate off her finger, pressed the green button. "Hansen here, hello ..."

"Volker Kroeger from the Hamburg Criminal Investigation Department. Am I speaking to Irene Hansen?"

He knew exactly who he had called. Did his communication manual tell him to reassure himself? "Yes, I'm Irene Hansen," Irene said.

"I am still busy with the investigation in the Hubert Hansen case." He paused, probably to give her time to listen to his request.

So Hubert had become a 'case' by now, Irene thought bitterly.

"I have a question about that."

Why did this Kroeger make things so complicated? If he had questions, he should ask them.

Aloud, Irene said, "I'm listening."

"Did your husband take drugs?"

"What?" she gasped.

"Traces of narcotics, cocaine to be precise, have been found in the car."

"That can't be. My husband didn't take drugs." Her brain raced. She said it so categorically, but with everything she had learned about Hubert so far: did she really know for sure that Hubert had not become intoxicated.

Kroeger was already talking further. "I didn't claim that either. No residue was found in the remains of his body. But cocaine was transported in the car. That's quite certain."

All sorts of things flashed through Irene's mind. None of it seemed to make sense. She clung to one idea: "Was it even our car? The Porsche?"

Volker Kroeger sounded pitiful. "HH-HH 1. The body number is also correct. Unfortunately unambiguous."

"Yes, that's Hubert's car." He had paid a small sum to get exactly this number plate: Hamburg - Hubert Hansen - number one. At the time, she had smiled at the little vanity. Had also been a little proud of the sleek car. Desperately, Irene searched for a topic that had nothing to do with drugs. She would face this new, terrible truth later. Maybe Madlen had taken coke? That would fit this tramp more than Hubert. Did the young girl need the help of chemical substances to get involved with a man who could be her father? But Hubert had been good-looking, Irene thought.

As Kroeger cleared his throat, she remembered that she was in the middle of a phone call. She remembered that the police officer didn't know anything about Madlen yet.

She said, "I can now tell you the name of the woman who witnessed the accident. Madlen." Feverishly she thought about what the surname had been. Something that didn't sound like Hamburg, but .... "Wrobel. Madlen Wrobel. She should be back in Hamburg by now."

"What do you mean again?"

"She showed up here and made a scene for me. Apparently she was more closely acquainted with my husband." She choked out the words.

"I see." Volker Kroeger abstained from commenting. "We'll find her, no problem. Are you sure it's the witness who was in the car with your husband?"

"Yes, she told us what happened." Irene tried to put the images of a gunshot to the head and a burning car out of her mind. "She was apparently in shock, but we advised her to come to you to make a statement."

"That's good. We'll find her anyway, now that we have the name. Thank you for your help. And if you remember anything about how the cocaine got into your car ... You have my number. If I'm not available myself, leave a message with a colleague and I'll get back to you." Kroeger said goodbye and ended the connection.

Irene exhaled audibly. She leaned back. "Do you have any more chocolate?"

CHAPTER THIRTY-THREE

IRENE LOOKED IN THE MIRROR. There were deep shadows under her eyes. She had tossed and turned all night, thinking about whether she should book a last-minute flight to Hamburg and accompany Suzie. But somehow she couldn't bring herself to do it.

Then she had driven to Barcelona airport, accompanied Suzie to the gate and returned. Actually, she was exhausted and would have preferred to end the day with a glass of wine. But she had an appointment with Pep. It was only in two hours - people here ate later than in Germany. Then she would be even more tired.

She thought about cancelling. But then she could have flown to Hamburg right away. She would lie down for half an hour, then drink a coffee and simply put make-up over her tiredness.

When the alarm clock on her mobile phone rang, she was even more ready than before. It took some effort to drown out the blue shadows under her eyes with concealer. In the end, she still found herself unflattering, but saw no way to improve anything. She put on three different blouses until she decided on one that went well with her brown eyes and emphasised her neckline without looking too revealing.

Finally she stood at the pier where they had arranged to meet. Her heart was beating up to her neck. Just like when she had met Hubert as a teenager. Was she about to cheat on him now?

Before she could lose herself in musings, she saw the tall figure of Pep strolling along the promenade. She pushed away all thoughts of Hubert and decided to allow herself only positive thoughts tonight.

Pep greeted her again with kisses on the cheeks.

"Where is Fosca?", Irene asked in greeting and immediately scolded herself that this was not the most charming start to an evening together.

"At my sister's. It's actually her dog." Pep hooked up with her and led her to the restaurant, which was hidden on the pier at the fishing harbour. She would never have dared to enter this part of the harbour, which seemed to be reserved for fishermen, if the signage was to be believed. The 'Confraria', that is, the 'Brotherhood of Professional Fishermen' ran the place, as Pep explained. It had existed for decades and processed the freshly caught fish from the cutters.

The food was excellent, there was a choice of different fish. The prices for a single course corresponded to what Irene spent when she went out for a pizza with Suzie in Hamburg. She had to admit that the culinary pleasure here was incomparably higher. And secretly expected Pep to foot the bill. The thriftiness she had cultivated all her life could not be discarded from one day to the next, even if she had inherited. It had not yet turned out exactly how much the amount was.

When dessert was served, a pleasant tiredness enveloped Irene. The exhaustion of the afternoon had disappeared. In her mind, she let the day pass before her eyes once more. The hustle and bustle of the many people at the airport - it had reminded her of something, she just didn't know what. Maybe she was no longer used to such a hustle and bustle because of the many walks on the beach. But then an image flashed through her mind: Pep holding up a sign saying *M. Van* when she had picked Suzie up from the airport. It had been lurking in the back of her mind all along.

"The van Vreeden, what was he doing here?"

"Van Vreeden? That was a colleague of your husband's from the office in Hamburg."

"I know that. What is he doing here?"

Pep looked at her attentively. "He wanted to see if we could develop relations between the Hamburg office and us. At least that's what he said."

Irene heard an undertone. "You don't believe him?"

Pep hesitated, then said: "Sounded like a pretext. He was very intensely interested in a single project. Which surprises me, because that has long been completed, both in terms of building permits and construction progress. And we have new projects going on with the Hamburgers in the meantime."

"What kind of project?"

"I shouldn't talk about my work, but since your husband also worked on it, I guess it's not much of a secret. The Hamburg office was in charge of a hotel construction in Salou. Here in the neighbouring town."

Irene remembered. The constant trips to Spain had started with the hotel in Salou. Hubert had been under more and more stress, even the little time they had had together until then had fallen victim to the study of building documents and the constant journeys. If only he had at least flown, but because of his fear of flying he had driven by car, always two days each way.

With the hotel construction, the architecture firm had really taken off. Follow-up orders in Spain had rained in. Had it really been worth it, Irene asked herself. "What does van Vreeden want with this hotel now? It's already finished, as far as I remember."

"Yes, an investor has come in. Big deal. We were paid well and the Hamburgers also made their cut. I don't know why, but van Vreeden went to my boss and asked for all the documents we had. Then he locked himself in a private office and went through everything. He thought everything was perfect, thanked me and left again.

At that moment the waiter came and asked if they wanted a coffee.

After the multi-course meal, Irene could use some stimulation, even though she had already had a coffee in the afternoon. She ordered a cortado, an espresso with milk, Pep took a café solo, espresso without milk.

He leaned forward and let his hand rest on the table, right next to

Irene's hand, so close that they touched very lightly. "That was a nice evening."

Irene managed to nod. The impulse to pull her hand away was only very brief. Stronger was the desire to take his hand. She couldn't do that, but she turned her arm a tiny bit so that she felt Pep a tiny bit stronger.

He had obviously noticed that she was coming towards him and now placed his hand on hers. His warmth flowed through her. She did not dare to move. Enjoyed the touch.

Then the coffees were served. They withdrew their hands, raised their cups and looked into each other's eyes.

Irene would have liked to hold on to this moment forever, but it passed. They finished their drinks. Pep paid the bill, they walked back across the pier. On the one hand, Irene was glad that Pep made no further advances, but on the other hand she longed for the warmth of his body.

They walked along the harbour promenade. The closer they got to Irene's flat, the more fears rose in her. Now she would have to spend the night alone and the door had not yet been repaired. Because of the weekend, Carlos had not been able to find a workman to repair the burglary damage.

"What's wrong?" Pep seemed to sense her tension.

Irene took a deep breath and described what had happened. The break-in, the wild search, the damage to the flat. Finally, she told him about the cheap mobile phone with the many SIM cards.

"You called there?" Pep raised his eyebrows. "And it was a Latino on the line? From which country, did you recognise the dialect?"

She just shook her head.

"Colombian, maybe."

She shrugged her shoulders. She couldn't tell the South American dialects apart. Besides, she had other worries. A shame such as she had never experienced before nested inside her. She felt ashamed, though there was no reason for it. Abysmally ashamed to have got into such a mess. Until now, her life had been manageable and controlled. If there were problems, she had worked hard to solve them. But now she was in a situation from which she saw no way out. The easiest thing would be to fly back to Hamburg. But that would be a surrender and was out of the question.

She felt this anger inside her. She finally wanted to know what had happened between Hubert and her in the last few years. When had it started, that he led a parallel life of which she knew nothing? What had triggered their estrangement? She had lied to herself all these years. Or simply seen the good in their marriage, looked past the contradictions and apparent trivialities. She would never let that happen again, she swore to herself.

As these thoughts flashed through her mind, tears welled up in her eyes.

Pep took her in his arms and rocked her very gently back and forth. He wiped her tears with one thumb. It felt like a feather was touching her face, he was so careful.

She sobbed out once more.

Finally, Pep gave her a hug and said, "You don't have to sleep here. Come to my place!"

CHAPTER THIRTY-FOUR

IN THE DARK, it was not so clear how big the villa was, but it seemed huge. It was set back from the road, between mighty pine trees. Further ahead were gnarled almond trees. There was a whiff of almond blossom in the air that reminded her of her trip yesterday.

Pep had his arm around Irene's shoulders as they walked to his estate. That felt reassuring and strengthening. Irene was ashamed of her tears by now.

But she forgot what had happened when Pep led her into his house. The imposing interior distracted her from her grief. Through a long hallway they came into a living room with floor-to-ceiling windows. The load-bearing beams could be seen on the ceiling, giving structure to the whole room. Modern paintings brought colour into the room. A sofa and several comfortable-looking armchairs stood in front of a fireplace.

"A fireplace, how great."

"It gets quite cold here in winter." Pep hinted at a shiver.

"What you call cold," Irene laughed, thinking of the endless grey winter days with drizzle in Hamburg.

"Make yourself comfortable!" Pep pointed to the sofa.

Irene dropped into the cushions and watched as Pep put a few logs in the fireplace, stuffed paper underneath and lit it. Soon the first flames rose. In no time at all, a pleasant warmth spread.

"Would you like a drink?"

Irene was still tipsy from the wine at dinner, but a nightcap never hurt, right? She nodded.

Pep went to the kitchenette, which was separated from the living room by a counter. Like in her flat, only everything was much bigger. Stainless steel flashed in the kitchen, as Irene noticed out of the corner of her eye. She stood up and looked around curiously.

Her gaze fell on the painting above the sofa. Strong brushstrokes indicated a rider. Saint George with his lance, the slain dragon under the hooves of his horse.

"Sant Jordi, the national saint of the Catalans," Pep explained. He with came two drinks to her.

She remembered the medieval-looking town of Montblanc, where the knight and his dragon had been omnipresent. "A people who worship a dragon slayer. They must be people who fear nothing."

Pep smiled mischievously. He pressed one of the glasses into her hand.

They sat down next to each other on the sofa. Irene pushed all her worries aside and snuggled close to Pep. It just felt good.

Pep put his arm around her. Then he put his drink on the coffee table and pulled her closer to him. He moved closer to her face, looked into her eyes.

She lowered her eyelids and looked at his full lips, which were seductively close. She would only have to lean forward a little and ...

At that moment, Pep kissed her. Cautiously probing at first, then more and more boldly.

It felt incredible. She pushed herself towards him and opened her mouth.

He broke the kiss, looked deep into her eyes. "We are crazy," he murmured and lowered his lips to hers again.

Unfamiliar feelings stirred in her belly. She felt safe and protected from all the trouble in the world. She pushed all thoughts away and let herself sink into the cushions of the sofa. Concentrated on the warmth of his lips, the exploratory movements of his tongue and those incredible blue eyes.

At that moment she heard footsteps. Rustling of clothes.

They sat up.

Over Pep's shoulder she saw a woman. An elegant woman, about fifteen years younger than her. Under her summer dress, a baby bump was clearly visible.

CHAPTER THIRTY-FIVE

IRENE DREW in her breath in horror. A cold knife cut through her heart.

She pushed Pep back.

He struggled up from the sofa.

The strange woman stared at the two of them. "Bueno, I must have come at the wrong moment. Hello everyone!" She looked quite relaxed.

"Ana ..." Pep's voice was rough.

Irene stood up and smoothed out her clothes. She staggered to the door.

"Wait. I can explain everything." Pep hurried after her.

Irene grabbed her jacket and went to the front door.

"It's not what you think." Pep reached out but did not dare touch her.

Irene did not answer, she let the front door slam shut behind her. Lamps flared up in the garden, apparently activated by motion detectors. She left the property, orientated herself briefly and went to her flat. A taxi was nowhere in sight, and besides, it felt good to walk. It was cooler than it had been before ... how long had it been since they had left the restaurant? An hour perhaps? No matter, she pulled her jacket tighter around her shoulders, hurried across the harbour promenade and finally climbed the stairs to her flat.

The sight of the broken door did the rest. She sobbed. She rushed into the flat and curled up on the sofa. Cried and cried. Eventually, the tears stopped coming. She lay frozen for a while, then groped into the bathroom, stood under the shower and let warm water run over her body. Slowly she regained consciousness.

That whole trip to Cambrils had been madness. She had failed all along the line. She would return to Germany right away and try to forget what had happened. To push the blue eyes and the warmth of Pep's body out of her memory.

She dried off, dressed - this time choosing practical travel clothes - threw her personal belongings into the suitcase and wheeled it to the rental car. When she started the engine, the display announced that it was three in the morning. She was less tired than adrenaline-soaked, the many coffees did the rest.

She stepped on the gas and left Cambrils behind, turned up a radio station blaring flamenco tunes and forbade her brain to recapitulate the past hours and days.

She reached the airport in the record time of one and a half hours, parked the rental car in the car park, threw the key into the rental company's designated letterbox and went into the terminal ...

Only to find that the Lufthansa counter was still closed. She sat down on one of the benches, fiddled around on her mobile phone without understanding what she was reading. Then she sent a message to the broker asking him to lower the purchase price for the flat to an amount that seemed realistic to him. Finally, she nodded off. The bustle of an airport coming to life woke her up.

She staggered sleepily to the counter, got a ticket for the next flight, struggled through the controls and the aisle of duty-free shops until, after more waiting, she was finally seated. When the plane took off, she breathed a sigh of relief.

Only look forward, not into the past, she admonished herself, leaning back and trying to loosen her tense shoulders.

She didn't spare a glance for the sea over which the plane made an elegant turn shortly after take-off.

CHAPTER THIRTY-SIX

"WHAT ARE YOU DOING HERE?" Pep stared at Ana. They had often argued, rather listlessly; now, for the first time, he felt real anger rising.

"You're always alone. I didn't mean anything by it. Sorry if I interrupted." She said it lightly, as if it was a formality to apologise.

"You wanted to come back from Barcelona tomorrow." He wanted to talk it out now, doggedly pursued. "Why aren't you with ..." The name of her lover did not escape his lips.

"I'm pregnant, in case you haven't noticed." She sighed. "My back hurts. I took today off, went to gymnastics for mums and then out with a friend." She sat down on the sofa, jerked her heavy body around and put her legs over the back of it. "Sorry I was so late."

As if that were an excuse. She could have let us know beforehand. Pep grabbed her jacket, which she had put on a chair, and tossed it to her. "Out!"

She stared at him, aghast.

"This is my house too. You can't just kick me out like that." Protectively, she put her hands on her huge baby bump. "It's the middle of the night, where am I supposed to go?"

Pep sighed. "Then I'll go. When I come back, you'll be gone. You have exactly until ten o'clock to leave."

He left the house they owned together. He would have to sell it to pay off Ana. Good thing, that would also take away the memories of countless arguments. He was only sorry to have to leave the garden to someone else. Already he saw himself squatting in a tiny bachelor pad, alone.

It was dark. He heard the sea, but saw only a dark expanse to his left. In the meantime, he had walked along the beach promenade without being aware of where he was going. Just ahead was Irene's flat. He didn't want to think about her now either. He turned on his heel, walked back to his house and sat in the car. Better than a park bench. He remembered his grandparents' cottage. He started the engine.

After half an hour he reached the Pallissa. The torch he kept in the car for emergencies lit his way through the trees. He picked the key for the padlock from his waistband and opened it. Stale, humid air hit him.

There was a thick layer of dust on the table. He hadn't come here for ages, and Montse apparently had no interest in the grounds either. From a chest in the corner he fetched the hammock he had deposited there as a youth. The cheap nylon thing was fortunately indestructible. He searched and found the hooks he had wedged between the quarry stones back then. Then he went back to the car, got a fleece blanket out of the boot. He made himself as comfortable as possible in the hammock. His back was no longer as elastic as it used to be and it took him time to find a position that allowed his body to relax.

But his mind could find no peace. Incessantly he played the kiss for him, the horrified look of Irene on Ana's stomach and her hasty departure.

Pep rolled from side to side, each time rocking the hammock violently.

He had blown it. The one woman who listened to him, with whom he could not only talk but even keep quiet, he had driven into flight. First thing tomorrow he would call her and make it clear that he had nothing more to do with Ana. There had to be a way to win Irene back. With this confident thought, he finally fell asleep.

CHAPTER THIRTY-SEVEN

"MUM!" Jasmin flew around her neck. "Where did you come from?"

Irene pressed her daughter against her. She smelled good. Familiar. Then they detached from each other.

"You've got a tan!" Then Jasmin looked more closely at her. "Is something wrong?"

Irene felt as rumpled as she probably looked. She had slept through the flight, then taken a taxi home, felt strange there, and changed quickly to go to the hotel. Now she was standing here and didn't know what to do with herself. At first glance, everything appeared normal. Jasmin was obviously managing without her. She sat at the computer and checked the bookings.

As always, thought Irene. If there were still rooms available, she would offer them at a knockdown price. Undercut the other hotels to have a full house.

"Are you all right?" Her daughter's voice interrupted her thoughts.

"I'll tell you later." Irene wasn't sure she even wanted to tell Jasmin what had happened in Cambrils. It would be best if she left it at the bare facts about the property market. There was no way she would mention Pep. She would banish his name from her memory forever and ever. Just now he had tried to call her, whereupon she had blocked his number and deleted it from the address book. Let him keep his excuses to himself. She had seen enough.

"What is the flat in Cambrils like?" Jasmin was bursting with curiosity. "You said you were only going to stay for a few days? Was there much to sort out?"

"Nothing special." She wanted to preserve the image of an exemplary father for her daughter. She didn't need to know about a love nest full of cash, mysterious mobile phones and burglaries.

"Mum, on a different note, the police called several times and wanted to talk to you. I tried to reach you, but..."

"This Kroeger called me, I've already spoken to him." Irene didn't want to explain to her daughter that it was about murder and cocaine. She remembered Jasmin's many calls. If only she had answered. She probably would have returned to Hamburg days ago and saved herself the disaster with Pep, the man whose name she wanted to forget. The flat had to be sold as soon as possible. Hopefully the estate agent would get rid of it soon. Then the buyers would have to deal with burglaries.

She felt hot. She had forgotten the cash in the fridge! In her hurry to get away from Cambrils, she hadn't thought about it at all. It was an unreal sum for her anyway, more like a pile of paper than real money. As long as she didn't know where it came from, who it belonged to and what it was for, she wouldn't touch it. Especially since the bank would ask questions if she deposited such a sum into their account. Before that, the cash would have to be declared to customs. The posters detailing this regulation had been impossible to miss at the airport. Should she smuggle the notes into Germany? She had no intention of abandoning the money. She saw it as a kind of compensation for her problems. Especially since anyone who found it would ask questions about her. Questions she couldn't answer. She would have to return to the flat one last time to get the money.

"The police insisted on seeing you in person. Otherwise they told me they were going to send a summons." Jasmin sounded worried.

"I'll take care of it."

Jasmin pulled her into the breakfast room, to a table they only set when the hotel was completely booked, because it was in a dark corner.

"Look."

With a grand gesture, she pointed to the table that was set for breakfast. However, the cheerful bright orange paper napkins were missing. Instead, a grey cloth napkin, artfully folded, lay on the plate. The white earthenware had been exchanged for another set, a beige-grey one. Her daughter beamed at her.

"Isn't it great?"

"Looks, um, restrained."

Irene made an effort to compliment her proud daughter, though she didn't know what for.

"A little touch of colour would brighten it up."

"Oh mum! Leon designed this, he's a graphic designer. Our followers on Instagram loved it."

With a flourish, she opened the cloth napkin and held it out to Irene.

"Real linen, feel it!"

Irene took the cloth in her hand and felt it.

"Quite scratchy and stiff."

"They get buttery soft when you've washed them more than once. Washing them saves a lot more resources compared to the disposable napkins."

Jasmin took a deep breath.

"The idea is to make the hotel carbon neutral. We would be the first carbon neutral house in the place."

She looked at Irene.

"Child, it all costs money ..."

"The life insurance will pay..."

"The heating needs to be replaced urgently. It's banging in the winter."

"That would be part of the plan. The old heating system not only bangs, it also consumes far too much fossil fuel. Solar power and infrared heating would be much better. Leon and I have written a business plan. The bank has shown initial interest. Mum, we need your signature.

Irene felt caught off guard. No sooner had she left for a few days than Jasmin had turned everything upside down. She promised Jasmin that she would look at documents. But she couldn't muster the enthusiasm her daughter apparently expected. She felt as if she needed to sleep for at least three days in a row. But getting any rest looked unlikely.

"I'll look at it."

She folded the linen napkin and put it back on the table. Then she slumped down on a chair.

"Will you bring me a coffee?"

CHAPTER THIRTY-EIGHT

IRENE STRODE through a long corridor in the Hamburg police headquarters. In the ultra-modern building in the shape of a ship's hull, she looked for Volker Kroeger's office. Finally, she asked a woman pushing a trolley full of files in front of her, and she directed Irene to a room hidden in a corner just beside the stairwell.

She knocked and entered the room after hearing "come in". A stocky man with grey temples, about her age, looked at her attentively. He held out his hand, gave hers a firm squeeze, and then pointed to the chair in front of his desk. Piles of paper were piled up next to his computer, with colourful sticky notes poking out of them.

Kroeger's alert eyes betrayed intelligence. He summarised what she already knew. Hubert had been shot from a passing car, then the perpetrators had stopped, doused the car with petrol and set it on fire. An unknown woman had managed to escape from the car.

"As I said, I know who this woman is. It is Madlen Wrobel."

"How do you know?"

Irene swallowed, then pulled herself together.

"She was my husband's mistress."

She watched Volker Kroeger sharply, but he didn't bat an eyelid. In his position, the man has probably already seen everything there is to see in life, Irene thought to herself. She told him how the woman had appeared in her life, but did not mention that she had claimed the money and the flat for herself. She described the woman's emotional breakdown and how she had explained the attack on the car.

"This sequence of events is consistent with our investigation findings."

Kroeger scribbled on another sticky note. It seemed to be his system of order. Then he cleared his throat.

"I'm glad you could come in person. I have unpleasant news for you. Unfortunately, we have had to temporarily freeze all accounts in your husband's name. Even though you have received the certificate of inheritance, you cannot withdraw anything from these accounts at the moment."

"Why?"

Irene felt rattled. She had got up early to drive to the north of Hamburg, where the Criminal Investigation Unit resided in the local police headquarters. From the bright sun of Catalonia, she had landed under the grey skies of the Hanseatic city to falling drizzle. Irene's shoulder had started to ache again. She would have liked a coffee to get her circulation going, but Kroeger hadn't offered her one.

"This has to do with the ongoing investigation."

"Is our joint account also affected?"

They had had two separate accounts, one for the hotel, the other for Hubert's income from the architecture firm. That seemed cleaner and easier for them to keep track of. Only the funds they needed for expenses each month were in the joint account. From the beginning of their marriage, Hubert had insisted that each of them also keep a personal account for "the little luxuries that they allowed themselves". Except that Irene's private account was always in the red.

"We have already checked and released the joint account so that you can continue to pay your expenses. More interesting are your husband's other accounts. Among them are wallets for cryptocurrencies. Here we are still working on gaining access. Do you have access to the passwords at all?"

"Cryptocurrencies?"

Irene had an unclear idea what that meant. Words like 'darknet' and 'Bitcoin' buzzed through her head without her being able to make any sense of them. Hadn't Madlen claimed that Hubert had owned Bitcoin?

"They consist of twelve English words per account."

"Twelve?"

Her own passwords consisted only of a single sequence of letters and numbers, for which she had created mnemonic devices so as not to forget them. Jasmin's birthday, the day of her wedding ...

"So-called seed phrases. Twelve unrelated English words. Does your husband perhaps have a notebook somewhere with the passwords?"

She shrugged helplessly. Jasmin had big plans for the hotel. For that they would need the inheritance, and all of it. The money from Hubert's accounts. The notary had rattled off a six-figure sum when discussing the will, which would definitely be enough. Then there was the life insurance and the proceeds from the sale of the flat in Cambrils. A stab went through her heart again at the thought. But she forced herself to concentrate on her present problems.

"I'm afraid I can't help you there. I don't understand why the accounts were frozen anyway. Hubert is the ... victim."

She struggled to get the words out. She still couldn't believe that someone had shot Hubert. Something like that only happened in the cinema, not in real life, not in venerable Hamburg.

Volker Kroeger slid back and forth on his chair, scratching his nose.

"There are indications that Hubert Hansen was involved in criminal activity."

"Please, he was an architect."

Volker Kroeger put his hands together. "Let's add it up: Someone shot him dead, cocaine was being transported in his car. He probably owned cryptocurrencies, at least we were able to prove that he had installed the necessary wallets. That in itself is not reprehensible, but all taken together ..." He let the sentence hang in space.

Irene lowered her head. In the last few days and especially nights, she had done nothing but think about Hubert's secrets. She had to stop kidding herself: Hubert was involved in something that didn't seem legal. She had briefly considered whether one of the builders had disliked a design. But that was hardly a reason for an attack.

"He owned a flat in Spain that he never told me about," she added. She reported on the searches.

Volker Kroeger listened to her with a furrowed brow.

Then she opened her handbag and took out the mobile phone she had found in the flat together with the SIM cards. She had taken it with her, but had not known what to do with it until just now. Kroeger with his level-headed manner instilled her with confidence. She would give it to him, after all, he was the policeman. If he had to deal with the mobile phone and the mysterious caller, she would be rid of the problem. She would sell the flat in Cambrils, donate Hubert's suits to a charity and then move on. She had to take care of the hotel. Jasmin could take over, whispered a voice inside her that she immediately suppressed.

She put the mobile phone on the table, pushed it over to Kroeger and told him about the caller with the South American accent.

"A Latino?" The wrinkles on Kroeger's forehead deepened. "And he said he would call again?"

"Something like that. He told me to keep the phone, that he'd contact me." She didn't tell Kroger about the phrase "You have something that belongs to us." She didn't want to tell him about the cash, for whatever reason. Was she corrupt too? With the money she could take a trip to the Seychelles, buy a new car or simply modernise the dilapidated heating system in the hotel. Anyway, she saw it as compensation for all the grief, disappointment and shame she had gone through in the last few weeks. It was hers, full stop.

Kroeger looked at the mobile phone. "There will probably be no fingerprints we can identify because you've had it in your hand, several times. I'll give it to the tech anyway, just in case something does turn up."

He sighed as if he didn't have much hope. Irene thought, had Suzie also touched the phone? Not according to her memory. That's when she heard Kroeger say that she had to give her fingerprints so that the technicians could rule them out.

"I'll take you to the officer who does that later. Or have you already been treated for identification? Then you can save yourself the procedure."

Irene shook her head. She had never come into contact with the police at all, except for that stupid rear-end accident decades ago. She had certainly never had to give her fingerprints. She would remember that.

"Does anyone in Spain know that you are back in Hamburg?"

Irene thought about it. She had left in a hurry at night. No one knew of her departure. Carlos would notice after some time.

"My neighbour probably ..."

Kroeger sighed again.

Just then, Irene's phone rang. She was annoyed that she hadn't switched it off. *Suzie* appeared on the display. She ignored the call.

"Go ahead and answer it, we're done here. Thank you for your help."

She couldn't image how she had aided the investigation.Kroeger accompanied her to a corner office on the ground floor, where a grumpy guy was sitting, who pressed her fingers one by one onto a scanner. The black ink thing you saw on TV was probably obsolete. Irene felt like a criminal when the man pressed her fingers with a firm grip on the smooth surface of the machine.

CHAPTER THIRTY-NINE

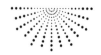

IRENE WALKED along the Alster to clear her head. The water lay flat, hardly distinguishable from the pale sky, had it not been for the line of houses on the bank. A lone rower glided through the water, pulling the oars rhythmically.

Drizzle wet Irene's face. She pushed the hood further into her forehead. Her shoulder still ached.

The telephone rang. Suzie again.

"Have you got time for lunch?"

"Sure. Let's meet at the museum café."

"Oh yes, I love the starter plate!"

Suzie was so lucky. She could always eat, no matter what time of day. No matter what, without gaining weight. Her yoga exercises probably contained a secret fat burning booster.

Irene hung up and continued walking. She stepped into a puddle that it soaked the hem of her trousers. Water penetrated one of her shoes and squelched with every step.

She felt so clumsy. In contrast to Suzie's slender yoga body, she put on fat, had wrinkles on her neck like a turtle, and her joints ached. No wonder Pep - no, she would only call him Josep Folch i Bosch now - only wanted to eat her up as a nice side dish. She was sure he dallied with all his clients. And his wife was pregnant. How disgusting that he cheated on her. Wait a minute, he wasn't really cheating on her, they hadn't got that far. Would the kiss have led to more?

Unexpectedly, she had reached the Ethnological Museum at Rothenbaum, which was now called 'Cultures and Arts of the World'. The term 'ethnology' was no longer politically correct, but the content of the museum remained: works of art and everyday objects from the history of Latin America, Polynesia and Africa. When she had time to wander through the rooms, Irene couldn't get enough of the blaze of colour and the diverse patterns on textiles and wickerwork. She always returned invigorated from a tour of the museum, just a few minutes' walk from her hotel.

Now she entered the magnificent entrance and went to a side door behind which was the restaurant and café. The waitress greeted her in a friendly manner. Irene looked for a table at the back against the wall. No sooner had she taken a seat than Suzie rushed in. Somehow, she always managed to make a grand entrance. Today she had jazzed up her plain jeans and turtleneck with a colourful silk scarf.

She pressed kisses to Irene's cheeks and sat down.

"Two lattes please, then the starter plate. A glass of red?" Suzie looked at Irene.

"It's too early."

"You're right," Suzie said resignedly. She ordered a bottle of water and two glasses. Suzie turned to her friend.

"Why aren't you in the sunny south?" she said. "You told me you wanted to stay. What brought you here all of a sudden?"

Irene bit her lip. Then she told Suzie everything.

"Pregnant? Are you sure?"

"You couldn't miss it."

She could have kicked herself. How could she be so idiotic as to fall for a man? To blindly trust blue eyes? Soon she would be checking out and stalking anyone who made the slightest advances. Or better still, not get involved in anything at all. She was a widow. Didn't one have to wait for a year of mourning as a matter of decency anyway? Her feelings were unreliable. One day she mourned Hubert bitterly, one day she cursed him and his machinations, the next she snuggled up to Pep. She couldn't allow such emotional chaos, she reminded herself.

"Maybe it wasn't what you think ..."

"What else would it be like?"

Suzie didn't know what to say to that either.

The waitress brought the coffee. Next to each cup was a butter biscuit on the saucer.

Suzie dipped it into the liquid with relish.

Silently, Irene handed over her own biscuit. Her stomach was churning.

"Listen!"

Suzie's tone alerted Irene that she now had something important to say. She looked at her friend attentively.

"Carlos called me."

"He liked you, didn't he?"

Irene remembered her vision of the two of them stark naked on the beach doing yoga exercises. Only in her imagination of course, but the image persisted in her mind's eye.

"That's not the point. Anyway, he says that Pep asked about you. So, he's still interested in you."

"But I'm not interested in him."

Her voice sounded harsher than intended. Then she remembered Kroeger's question. 'Who knows about you leaving?' If Carlos knew she was back in Germany, he wasn't the only one. The maid and Juan would know. Carlos would have already told Juan to fix the door yesterday. Had he also told Pep that she had left? She remembered Volker Kroeger's furrowed brow.

"Maybe he just wants to know where I am."

"What makes you think that?" Suzie took a piece of baguette and dipped it in the aglio-olio dip.

"Maybe he's behind everything that's happened. The break-in and the searches."

"You're out of your mind. He's a Gestor in a prestigious consulting firm."

"So what? Hubert was also an architect in a prestigious office."

Irene pursed her lips. She had been living guilelessly with a man of whose life she had only seen a fraction. Cash in quantities, a secret flat, a mistress and, last but not least, a car in which drugs had apparently been transported. A lot had come together that she had not known. She would uncover step by step what Hubert had kept secret from her. And she would not fall for another man who hid something from her. A pregnant wife, for example.

"I don't trust anyone anymore!" she announced, banging on the table, making Suzie wince.

Did she just give her a pitying look? She could save herself pity, that was the last thing she needed. Irene reached for her handbag, dug out her wallet and announced that she would pick up the bill. After all, she had a secret stash of cash in Cambrils.

CHAPTER FORTY

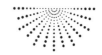

"I KICKED ANA OUT."

"Did you?" Xavi looked up. "About time." He moved aside folding chairs that were still standing around from the Colla's last rehearsal.

Pep squinted his eyes to keep from crying. He was no weakling. Maybe not an Iberian macho either, but he wouldn't cry. Not in front of his friend.

"What are you expecting? Now you seduce this German tourist and live in eternal happiness?"

The sarcasm in Xavi's voice was impossible to miss. Ever since Cap de Colla's childhood sweetheart had married someone else, he had had nothing but derision for the subject of love and relationships. Pep told him what had happened.

"She left."

Xavi pointed to the freezer in the next room. "Do you want a Coke?"

Pep nodded. He was glad of a distraction.

Xavi handed him a bottle. He said: "My advice: find a pretty Catalan girl and have fun."

"But I don't want a Catalan."

At that moment, Pep realised how much he longed for Irene. Being with her had felt good. Kind of like being wrapped in a warm blanket.

She liked order and punctuality, just like him. Maybe that was his German side. .

The meetings with Irene had felt easy. Nothing was stressful. She did not put herself in the centre, rather she listened to him attentively, gave him her ear. Ana had driven him crazy with her vague appointments, chaos in scheduling and constant delays.

But that was over now. Since Irene's hasty departure, she had not answered any of his messages, nor had he reached her by phone. Apparently, she had blocked his number. The flat in Cambrils was deserted. She must have returned to Germany. He was tempted to meet this Carlos and ask him out. Maybe he would borrow Montse's dog later and pass by the apartment complex quite by chance. Carlos always sat in the café downstairs at this time.

"New tourists come in the summer."

Xavi rolled up a black sash that one of the Xiquets had left lying around. Pep would have liked to strangle his friend. Did he not understand him or did he want to provoke him? He changed the subject.

"I need a new flat. The house has to be sold."

"Are you Gestor or not?"

Xavi was right. He knew exactly what steps he had to take to set everything in motion bureaucratically. He cursed himself for not having initiated it months ago. Then this situation would not have arisen. He had just been too lazy. Hadn't wanted to burden Ana during the pregnancy. Or did he still have feelings for her? Had he wanted to win her back? He listened inside himself, but nothing stirred. At least since Ana had been pregnant by her lover, he had known that there was no turning back. He had also been too lazy to deal with her before. He had to admit to himself that he had given up on the relationship with Ana a long time ago. Now it was high time to formally end it.

He pulled out his mobile phone and called the broker with whom his office had always worked.

CHAPTER FORTY-ONE

SHE HAD SAID goodbye to Suzie and was on her way to her hotel when the mobile phone in her pocket vibrated. She took it out and looked at the display. She knew the number only too well. Hubert? Nonsense, she scolded herself, it's his office. She took the call, her heart still trembling.

"Hello, Mrs Hansen? It's VHB."

VHB stood for Van Vreeden, Hansen, Backhoff. Backhoff who had founded it, had long since retired. Hansen had died. Nevertheless, the initials remained because the brand had been established, Irene knew that. The young girl from the reception continued, "I'll connect you with Mr van Vreeden." She didn't know the girl, they changed every few months. Probably the gentlemen architects didn't think it necessary to pay them decently. Hubert had always complained about how high the costs for rent and employees were. In the meantime, he had put aside a considerable sum - although Irene doubted that this money came from the architects' business.

Then the cultivated, friendly voice of Manfred van Vreeden reached her ear. "Good morning, Mrs Hansen. How are you?"

Bad, but she wouldn't say that. She rubbed her aching shoulder and muttered something.

"If you need help, I'm happy to be there for you. I owe that to Hubert."

Irene thanked him.

"After all, we worked together for years, not least on the big hotel project in Spain. If there's something to catch up on, formalities or sifting through documents, I'm happy to do it."

"Thank you very much, my notary has already made the necessary arrangements."

"Perhaps you need the expertise of an architect for some procedures? I'm happy to be at your disposal."

Irene had an idea. She asked van Vreeden if she could drop by for a moment.

"Why is that? The documents we have here only refer to his work."

"I'm missing some papers that have to do with our joint account." Irene was surprised how easily the lie came from her lips.

"We'll take care of his things for you. If we find anything personal, we'll send it to you."

He was in a hurry to say goodbye and hang up. She glanced at her mobile phone. She was irritated. Irene had entered the hallowed halls of VHB many times before, why was van Vreeden turning her away now?

CHAPTER FORTY-TWO

FORTUNATELY, van Vreeden was nowhere to be seen when Irene entered
the VHB office. It was located at a prime address near the Jungfernstieg
in a Gründerzeit building with opulent ornamentation on the façade.
Inside, the rooms were kept simple, but benefited from high ceilings
and artfully nested parquet flooring.

Mrs Lange was elegant as always. She greeted Irene with feigned
empathy, offered her condolences once more, and led Irene to Hubert's
office. She told her that the police had taken the laptop, nothing more.
The papers were untouched.

"I'm afraid I have to leave you now," said Lange.

It sounded like what it was: a formality. Of course, Lange was busy
and of course, Irene didn't need any help with what she intended to do.
She wasn't even sure what she wanted here yet.

Hesitantly, she approached the desk, an antiquarian monster of dark
wood, pretty much the only classic piece of furniture in the room.
Hubert had been beaming when he had discovered it in an antique shop.

"It makes an exciting contrast to my shelves."

They were made of white tubular steel and covered the two long
walls of the room. Irene let her fingers glide over the smooth wood of
the desk. It felt warm. The room smelled stale as no one had aired the

room, since it was now unoccupied. The thought flashed through Irene's mind briefly of who would replace Hubert in the future and whether his successor would then also sit at this desk ... then she suppressed the idea.

It was painful to realise how fast the world turned while she was still struggling to acknowledge the loss of Hubert. But the horrific discoveries of the last few weeks almost drowned out it out. She pulled herself together, and opened the window to let the air in. In the courtyard stood a huge plane tree, stretching it's still bare branches into the sky.

Irene stepped back into the room and sat down on the black leather chair behind the desk. She systematically pulled open drawer after drawer, only to discover that office supplies were stored here, from paper clips to packets of A4 paper. The most exciting thing she found was a silver case with a hip flask. She twisted it open and sniffed the liquid. It appeared to be whiskey. At this time of day, just early afternoon, she did not feel like drinking. She closed the flask again and put it back.

Then she glanced around the room. The shelves were filled with files, neatly labelled. Next to the year numbers were abbreviations designating individual building projects and plans, as Hubert had once explained to her. A complex internal system.

She left the room, found Frau Lange in a tiny kitchen staring at a microwave.

"Can you tell me what Hubert had been working on recently?"

Long looked at her impassively from behind her glasses.

"Everyone is involved with all the projects. That way each partner can supplement the other if someone gets sick or ..."

She made a vague gesture with her hand. She didn't want to say 'or dies' after all.

"What are the most important projects at the moment?"

"The residential project in Eimsbüttel, the deal in the Alte Land and the property on the former factory site where we are planning high-quality condominiums."

The woman spoke like an advertising brochure. The microwave pinged. Lange opened the door and pulled out a bowl of fast food.

"And in Spain? Hubert was travelling in Spain, wasn't he?"

"Oh yes, I almost forgot. The hotel in Salou. Huge deal."

Lange pointed to her food and left the kitchen. At the door she turned again and called out to Irene the abbreviation for the project in Salou. "ES-SAL-Ho."

With this new knowledge, Irene again turned to the monster of shelves in Hubert's office. *ES-SAL-Ho was* written on no less than three folders, which she heaved onto the desk. She leafed through them aimlessly. Unfortunately, she had never been interested in her husband's profession, which seemed richly technical to her. He, on the other hand, could never warm to the hotel business. Apart from when it came to building new properties, as recently in Spain.

In the first folder, ES-SAL-Ho, there were a lot of plans that covered the entire desk when unfolded. The hotel seemed to consist of partial complexes, at least she recognised floor plans for several buildings with several floors. In the second folder, she found Excel spreadsheets with calculations, from structural analysis to cost estimates and initial invoices. Irene choked when she looked at the sums in euros. She remembered how Hubert had always moaned that with all the high turnover, little was left for the architects. Maybe that was the case here too.

The third folder contained a lot of reports, filed chronologically and going back three years. Suddenly, Irene's gaze fell on the line *Client. Gonzalez S.A.* Next to it was an address in Cambrils. She pulled out her mobile phone and photographed it, as well as the last progress report. At that moment, someone cleared their throat behind her. She turned around. Michael van Vreeden was standing in the doorway. He was not alone. Next to him was a small black-haired woman with piercings on her face. She had one arm wrapped around van Vreeden's waist.

CHAPTER FORTY-THREE

HER EYES WENT BACK and forth between the two.

"That was quick," Irene finally said.

Van Vreeden patted Madlen's upper arm. He radiated pride of ownership. Then he frowned.

"I told you we would send you the personal effects."

He stepped closer and looked at the documents. Madlen stopped uncertainly at the door.

"The hotel in Salou? I'll take care of that now, it's all under control."

It sounded like a warning or was she imagining it? Van Vreeden folded the folder shut and put it back on the shelf, took the other two and slid them into the space next to it. "The police took all the documents. They were on the laptop. These are just printouts for our archives."

Irene understood that her presence was not wanted. She didn't know what else she wanted in the office. Therefore, she nodded at van Vreeden, ignored Madlen, took her coat and left. Before the office door closed behind her, she heard footsteps. Madlen was running after her.

"I was just leaving too," the young woman said. Her piercing sparkled.

"That was quick."

Irene could not suppress her remark. She wondered to herself how caustic her tone sounded.

"He's always been lusting after me."

Madlen was obviously proud of her conquest. Irene quickened her steps. She would be terribly happy to be alone now. Madlen also walked faster.

"I need a sugar daddy after all."

Irene shuddered at the name. Her Hubert, a sugar daddy? Wasn't that something that only existed in the USA?

"For my studies. I can't pay for it otherwise."

Again, Irene thought that there still was the possibility of trying honest work. She herself had not earned much during her training as a hotel manageress, but she had lived with her mother who for her part, had managed to get by after her husband had died of a heart attack at an early age. Irene only remembered her father from photos. Her mother had always tried to offer her daughter a good life, even if she had to help out in a restaurant on weekends in addition to her job as a typist.

"What are you studying?"

"Law. It's fucking hard."

Irene had always thought that you had to be intelligent to do law. But she had no idea about studying. Then she changed the subject:

"Did Hubert take drugs?"

"What makes you think that?"

Irene said nothing.

"No, he always hated it when I smoked a joint. Wouldn't take a single puff."

Hubert Hansen from the VHB office stoned? There was no way Irene could imagine that.

"And cocaine?"

"Irene, coke is more Manfred's thing. Why do you ask?"

It bothered Irene enormously that Madlen called her by her first name, but on the other hand they were closely connected. Through the same man.

"What's actually going on with the flat in Cambrils? When will you give me the new key?"

"What?" Irene gasped.

"I'm entitled to that. It is mine. And you still owe me the two hundred euros for the bikini."

"I sold the flat." As good as, Irene thought. "And I owe you exactly nothing." She turned on her heel and left.

CHAPTER FORTY-FOUR

IRENE CLOSED the door of the hotel behind her. She breathed a sigh of relief. She was glad to have given Madlen a piece of her mind.

In the breakfast room, Jasmin was sitting with a young man.

The man had put his long hair into a bun. She found this hairstyle hideous, which seemed to be chic among young men at the moment. The sleeves of his checked shirt were rolled up and showed forearms with full tattoos. Who had Jasmin picked up there?

"Hello," she said into the room.

"Mum, it's nice of you to come. This is Leon."

Leon nodded at her.

"Hello," she said again.

"We are doing a tasting right now," explained Jasmin.

There were many small bowls on the table.

Jasmin held out a spoon to her and pushed over three plates of a yellowish substance. "Taste it, which scrambled egg is better?"

Irene took a spoonful of the mixture and chewed on it. "Completely tasteless. These aren't organic eggs?"

"There are no eggs in it at all. It's vegan," said Leon, in a condescending tone.

"We want to be the first climate-friendly hotel in Hamburg. The vegan breakfast is just the beginning," said Jasmin.

Irene rolled her eyes. If the other dishes tasted anything like this rubbery, bland scrambled egg substitute, the hotel would be ruined. Jasmin pointed to the individual small bowls and explained: "Banana bread, tofu grilled cheese with tomato jam, pancakes with chocolate, fried mushrooms, rice paper bacon and vegan sausages - so we even have an English breakfast for those who like it hearty."

Irene sat down on a chair. "Do you think anyone will want to eat that?"

"Vegan is the new wave."

"Vegan food is much more climate-friendly than meat, milk and eggs." Leon sounded like a teacher. All he needed was to raise his finger.

"But you know how much our guests like eggs for breakfast. The scrambled eggs are always the first to go."

"They'll hardly notice the difference. Try this variation."

Jasmin pushed another plate towards her.

Sighing, Irene tasted her way through the selection. Some dishes tasted surprisingly good. She could get used to the avocado cream and the chocolate spread was delicious. The oat milk, on the other hand, was too slimy for her.

"It's a bit more expensive than our traditional breakfast, unfortunately, especially if you go for organic ingredients and fair trade," said Jasmin.

"As long as the accounts are frozen, we can't afford to experiment," Irene warned. Then she quickly looked over at Leon, but he didn't make a face. Had Jasmin already let him in on it? That was quick.

"Can't be long before they find out it was all a big mistake," Jasmin said lightly.

Irene pursed her lips. Fortunately, her daughter did not know what she had found out in the meantime. Hubert had definitely not been innocent, where else had the cash come from? And the drug traces in his car? There was no way she would discuss this in front of Leon. It was better for Jasmin to keep a wholesome image of her father anyway.

"And then the duvets," Leon said at that moment. "Down doesn't work at all."

"You want to change all the duvets?"

Irene counted up in her head how much that would cost.

"We have to find a suitable replacement first," said Jasmin, quashing her friend's enthusiasm.

Irene thought wistfully of the thick, expensive down duvets she had purchased for guests a few years ago. Female guests often thanked her for giving them warm feet at night.

She herself loved her down feathers, which retained the warmth even when she went to the toilet for a moment. Afterwards, she preferred to snuggle under their warmth.

"Think of how the poor geese suffer. They are plucked alive," Leon interjected.

Had he given Jasmin this idea about the climate-friendly hotel? Irene suddenly looked at the young man with different eyes. Was he a crazy radical who put fleas in her daughter's ear? Whereupon she would ruin the hotel with new-fangled ideas?

While she tasted more vegan appetisers, she reassured herself that the accounts were frozen anyway. Jasmin was only part owner and needed her signature if she wanted to take out a loan.

CHAPTER FORTY-FIVE

Pep nibbled on one of the tiny olives in the clay bowl in front of him. A light breeze made the midday heat bearable. Fosca had made herself comfortable at his feet. Her huge head rested on her front legs.

Miquel held his wine glass out to him invitingly. "Nice of you to remember me! It's been a long time since we've seen each other."

Pep raised his glass. They clinked glasses. A long time ago, indeed. Before he had married Ana, he had often gone out with Miquel. But the journalist had been too hard-drinking for him. It had always been late, the alcohol was always flowing.

Ana had been sitting at home waiting for him. Then the meetings with Miquel had become less and less frequent and finally stopped altogether. At some point they had lost sight of each other. But the mobile phone number that Pep had saved under 'Miquel' was still the right one.

"Are you a star reporter by now?" He smiled at his former friend.

"As if." Miquel took a big gulp. "Ah, this is a good one." He turned the bottle and looked at the label. "A Garnacha from Priorat, you can't go wrong with that."

The wine was heavy and velvety on the tongue. Pep briefly thought of the trip with Irene to the hinterland, when they had driven through the priory and admired the almond blossom. But he didn't want to remember that now. If he squeezed enough information out of Miquel, he would be able to help her - and win her back, he hoped. "Tell me, what do you do?"

"Got back to my Catalan roots." He mentioned the name of a nationalist daily newspaper that had been founded a few years ago. The main theme of the paper was to rail against the exploitation of Catalonia by the government in Madrid.

Pep raised his eyebrows. He had not previously placed Miquel in the Catalan camp, especially since the journalist had been born under the name 'Miguel' as the son of Andalusian immigrants. His father had slaved away in one of the countless car supply companies in Barcelona's industrial belt, his mother had sat at a supermarket checkout, and his eloquent son had eked out a living as a journalist.

Miquel shrugged his shoulders. "That's the only press that thrives. Otherwise, only tabloids sell. And television, you know, that's not my thing."

Pep nodded. Miquel was small and wiry, his mouth always a little pinched. He could not imagine him on the screen. Both men and women had to have a dentist's smile and model measurements to come across well.

Fosca growled menacingly when a woman with a poodle on a leash walked by. When Pep looked threateningly at his dog, he fell silent again. He knew that he wouldn't get any morsels from the table if he made a fuss.

The waiter approached their table. He knew Miquel, greeted him brightly, nodded to Pep and rattled off the dishes on the day's menu. Pep and Miquel decided on a light salad as a starter, and fish for the main course.

"How is Ana?"

"She's pregnant." It slipped out of Pep's mouth. Why had he said that? So far he had only given generally polite answers to enquiries to avoid discussions and gossip. Something had to have changed.

"Congratulations!" Miquel raised his glass.

"The child is not mine. We have separated."

"Oh, I'm sorry to hear that. I always thought you were a perfect couple."

I had seen it that way too, Pep thought bitterly.

"Who is the father then?"

"Her lover," Pep said curtly. It was clear that the journalist could not leave it at one question. He had to endure this inquisition, after all, he was the one who wanted something from him.

"Fling?"

Miquel smiled at the waiter who was serving the salads. Fresh greens, juicy tomatoes, crunchy cucumbers. It looked tempting.

"More like a long-term relationship that I didn't know about."

"How did that happen?" Miquel grinned. "Purely professional curiosity."

"She found a job in Barcelona, met this guy there and that was it. And she never wanted children..."

"I'm sorry." Miquel went to work on the salad.

"Don't be. I'll be fine."

Was he? Pep was glad that he could talk about the matter halfway emotionlessly. He didn't need to sugar-coat anything. Thousands of couples separated every year. Unlike in the Franco era, it was no longer a shame that had to be kept quiet and covered up.

Besides, he had met a great other woman. The thought brought him back to why he had wanted to meet Miquel.

"One of our clients is interested in the hotel project in Salou. You know, the new complex in the bay." He described the location. It wasn't a lie, surely Irene had an interest in what her deceased husband had built there. Could you say 'deceased' when someone had been shot? Dead was dead, Pep thought to himself.

"The hotel complex, yes, yes, I know what you're talking about." Miquel systematically speared lettuce leaves. "What's her interest in that thing?"

"A German architectural firm designed it."

"Planned and implemented. The Germans built and then sold."

Miquel pinched his mouth shut as if to stop himself from speaking further.

"So?", Pep inquired.

"Oh, haven't you heard from Don Enrique? Rumour has it that the project was not carried out with quite Germanic thoroughness."

"Why?"

"Some of the buildings were not finished when they were sold. They probably ran out of money. A building project like that always ends up being more expensive than planned. Cost explosion, you know."

"As architects, they should have known that. All building projects are more expensive than originally calculated."

Miquel shrugged his shoulders.

They drank wine in small sips, enjoyed the aroma.

"It's a great location, by the way. There's still something going on in Salou."

"Cheap tourism," said Pep contemptuously. The neighbouring town of Cambrils was unfortunately the scene of binge drinking. Tourists were brought in on buses or planes and stayed in cheap hotels to get sunburnt for a week and drink as much alcohol as possible. The latest scam was to jump from the balcony into the pool. Which often went wrong. Some posted spectacular pictures of so-called balconing, others never posted again.

"Not only. Salou has potential. The complex that the Germans have built looks sophisticated. At least the buildings that are finished. The price wasn't cheap either."

"How much did it cost?"

"Twenty million."

Pep swallowed. In his head, he counted up the offers he had read in the advertisements. He would get a real bargain with the flat he was thinking of buying. Property prices here on the coast were constantly high and still rising.

"It's nothing. Think of the transfer from the 'Star Hotel'."

Miquel nodded. "Keep in mind, however, that only part of the price is communicated publicly."

"There must have been a case of cash changing hands."

"On the other hand, they were Germans who built it." Miquel waved his fork to emphasise his point. "They are square heads, they calculate to the cent."

Pep thought of the strange things Irene had said about Hubert. The house search and the call from the Latino. Something had not gone right with the German architects. Square head, my ass.

The waiter came and cleared the empty salad plates.

"If it wasn't Germans, would you guess tax avoidance?"

"It is not for nothing that Spain is the country in Europe with the most five hundred euro notes in circulation. Far more than would correspond to our share in terms of national income or population."

"Unfortunately, too few of them circulate with me." Pep knew the statistics Miquel was referring to. The press chewed over them at least once a year. Corruption scandals came to light with regularity, and not only in the construction industry.

Pep thought with horror about the real estate deals that lay ahead of him. This was not going to go on with Ana and him in the villa. Neither of them could pay off the other, so they had to sell the beautiful house. But he didn't want to wait until a buyer was found - who might then push cash across the table - but find something new for himself right now. Something smaller, for the transition, he told himself. But with a view of the sea, that was a must.

"There are traces of cocaine on a large part of the five-hundreds, an examination has shown." Miquel smiled sardonically.

Pep nodded. That was nothing new. Spain was at the crossroads between Latin America and Europe and on the drug transfer route from North Africa to the metropolises of the North. There was a lot of cash in circulation, mostly in large notes. Traces of cocaine were regularly found in the sewage.

The waiter approached her table and served the main course with a grand gesture. It smelled of garlic and parsley. The fish was attractively draped, a fried tomato and fried potatoes formed the side dish.

Pep had no appetite. He thought of dinner with Irene at the restaurant on the harbour pier. He longed for her bright laughter.

CHAPTER FORTY-SIX

IRENE WAS SITTING in her kitchen reading the newspaper. Outside it was dull and grey. She hadn't been able to bring herself to go to the hotel yet. If Jasmin had managed on her own for so long, she would survive a few more hours. Besides, Irene didn't feel like going through any more vegan experiments. Sooner or later they would have to discuss which direction the business should take. But today Irene didn't feel up to it. The events in Cambrils were still worrying her.

She skimmed the headlines. Her gaze lingered on one news item: *Drugs seized.* The customs investigation had found and seized two and a half tonnes of cocaine in a container from Paraguay in the port. The drugs were hidden in cans that were supposed to contain putty. The spokesman for the authority expressed pride in the success. *The street price for this quantity is in the billions.*

Irene took another sip of coffee. It tasted disappointing, even though she had ground and brewed the beans herself. She missed the strong taste of the roast that is common in Spain. Maybe she should look for a Spanish bar in Hamburg to fight her wanderlust.

To distract herself, she delved further into the newspaper article. The editor had placed an interview, with the head of a Hamburg drug help centre, next to the text about the drug find at the harbour. The social worker said that the price of a gram of coke on the street had not gone up. The confiscation had no influence on the price because even two tons was a small amount compared to what drugs were in circulation. Besides, the port is only one way cocaine entered the country. In addition to such large-scale imports, small quantities were imported daily, for which the drug mafia had recruited hundreds of helpers.

Irene frowned. This Kroeger from the Criminal Investigation Unit had claimed that traces of cocaine had been found in Hubert's car. Had drugs been imported with the car? By Hubert? He would have had plenty of opportunity on his trips to Spain and back. Had the police found out more in the meantime?

She reached for her mobile phone, searched for Kroeger's number in the call list.

The ringing tone sounded for the fourth time. Maybe he wasn't in the office? Then there was a crack on the line. "Kroeger, Hamburg Ciminal Investigation Unit. What can I do for you?"

The police, your friend and helper, thought Irene. She gave her name and greeted the inspector, whose voice immediately became a shade warmer.

"Mrs Hansen, how can I help you?"

"I would like to know if anything new has come up."

"Unfortunately, I cannot say anything about the ongoing investigation at this stage."

"I need to know who did this to my husband ... who did this to him."

"We'll find the culprit and you'll be able to put it behind you." Kroeger sounded as if he was talking to a kindergarten child. 'Everything will be all right' or something.

"That mobile phone I gave you, what happened to it? Did you find any fingerprints?" Stupid question, she scolded herself, there were probably her own and Hubert's on it.

"Unfortunately, nothing usable," said Kroeger. "One question: Do you know a Manuel Martinez?"

"I've never heard of him."

"Did your husband have any acquaintances from Colombia?"

"Colombia? No, why?"

"The SIM cards are registered in a name from Madrid. The data matches that of a man from Colombia. However, this man died ten years ago. The mobile phone is a so-called burner."

"We've never been to Latin America at all."

Hubert's fear of flying had made long-distance travel impossible. So, he certainly hadn't been there secretly without her. That's what she told Kroeger. He listened to her explanation, muttered a few words about not being allowed to tell outsiders the facts of the investigation and that there were no exceptions for relatives either, then he said goodbye.

Irene's head was buzzing. Colombia - there was something. Pep had asked her if the caller who had threatened her spoke with a Colombian accent. How had he come up with Colombians, of all things? And what had Hubert had to do with Latinos?

CHAPTER FORTY-SEVEN

PEP LOOKED at the posters in the estate agent's window. They showed houses with pools, flats in complexes with pools and country houses with pools. Prices had risen significantly since Ana and he - at that time their villa was in terrible condition - had bought it. Pep was sorry to sell a house he had put so much work into.

But the situation was untenable. He had lived with Ana for far too long without really noticing her. They had lived together, but had grown apart. He had to make a break, that was clear. His life would not move forward on its own.

He pushed open the door and greeted Toni Sanchez. He didn't like the slick guy very much, but he had been working with Don Enrique's law firm for a long time. When Pep's clients needed advice on real estate, he sent them here. Conversely, Toni recommended the Gestoria if a prospective buyer didn't want to get the necessary documents in person. Given the legwork required by Spanish bureaucracy, that was often the case.

Toni greeted him kindly - well, of course, thought Pep, he's hoping for new business - and offered him a coffee, which he gratefully accepted. Then Toni held out a plate of donuts to him, but he was put off by the glittery icing.

Sanchez shrugged his shoulders and went to work on the pastries himself. Now, in the late morning, many Catalans had their breakfast, consisting of sweet pastries and a coffee. Pep followed his mother's German tradition and had a hearty breakfast, but he could always have a coffee.

He complimented Toni on his modern office and asked about business.

The broker had nothing to complain about. Between bites of the sweet curls, he enumerated some recent deals. "The prices are going up," he grinned. With the prices, of course, his commission also increased.

"Commercial real estate, can you do it?"

"Do you want to invest?"

If Toni knew his bank balance, he wouldn't have asked that. As long as the villa was not sold, Pep could only afford a tiny flat, if at all. Still, he would be reluctant to rent. For one thing, supply was scarce. For another, any property, however small, would be an investment. Once the divorce and the sale of the villa were settled, which could take a year, then he would look for something suitable. And he would have already partially paid off the tiny flat he would occupy by then. He would then rent it out to tourists. At least that was the plan.

"Seriously, you make great returns in tourism," Toni interrupted his thoughts. He wiped the crumbs of the donut from his mouth. "I can only recommend it. Hotels are being built all the time, maybe you want to get in on a share of a project?"

"What about the new hotel in Salou?"

"What makes you think that? It's already sold."

"Heard, for twenty million."

Toni shrugged his shoulders. "Now the Colombians are renovating it, then they'll sell it for thirty. At least. Good deal."

"Colombian?"

"A Colombian company has struck a deal. The Germans had apparently run out of money. The construction was not finished. Therefore, the complex was available at a bargain price."

If the broker thought twenty million was a bargain, he had by now ascended to realms alien to Pep. He suppressed his unease and said only: "That's odd."

"It can happen. In construction, everything is always more expensive than planned. There are a lot of people earning money." Toni didn't seem surprised by the transaction. "This is a complex with several buildings. That's what people do now. One building was finished, the others still lacked electricity, interior finishing, etc. The Colombians are now doing something high-end. Four stars at least.

"What kind of Colombians are they?"

"Colombians, that's all." Toni shrugged his shoulders. "They own several hotels here on the coast. They're spreading out more and more. They've got plenty of money to spend."

Pep had a suspicion where the Colombian money came from, but did not want to discuss it with Toni. He asked about the agent's plans for the coming Easter week.

Toni beamed and told us that he had met a woman with whom he would fly to Mallorca. "Exclusive inland resort."

Pep was jealous for a moment. Toni always had some kind of women he went out with, mostly beauties like from a model catalogue. But his relationships don't last long, Pep consoled himself.

They chatted for a while longer.

As he was about to leave, Pep's eyes fell on an paper lying on Toni's desk. The photo on the front page looked familiar.

"May I?" He turned the sheet over, pulled it towards him and studied the text. *View of the marina, American kitchen, quiet location.* The property was all too familiar to him. An idea came to Pep.

CHAPTER FORTY-EIGHT

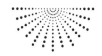

IRENE STARED out of the window into the grey of the Hanseatic weather. She couldn't bring herself to do anything. Actually, she had wanted to look for a new provider for the hotel's laundry service in order to negotiate a better contract.

Then the mobile phone had rung.

"I told you, at a realistic price you could get rid of the flat immediately."

The man sounded triumphant. When she heard the voice, Irene immediately pictured the young, lacquered estate agent who had surveyed her flat in front of her. Of course, he had to prove to her that his pricing policy had led to the goal. "Yesterday we were able to show your property to three interested parties. One of them has signed a preliminary contract and made a down payment in cash."

That had gone quickly. Irene thought for a fleeting moment of the mornings when she had sipped her coffee on the balcony and considered what colour the sea was showing today. The nuances in the blue-green of the waves had been there, tiny but noticeable. Every morning the sea had shown a different shade of blue.

"Okay?"

She had no idea what a pre-contract meant and asked.

"With the preliminary contract, the buyer secures the acceptance of the bid. If he withdraws after that, he loses his deposit. So, congratulations, madam. You've as good as sold the property. When can you come? We would schedule the notary appointment as soon as possible."

"I am flexible," Irene heard herself say.

"Then meet Mr Josep Folch i Bosch at the notary's office right away on Tuesday."

She gasped. This could only be a coincidence. "Josep Folch ...?"

"The buyer. Josep Folch i Bosch."

She made a gulping sound, then controlled herself and asked, "What about the other interested parties?"

"They tried to negotiate the price down. Their counter-offers were very low. Josep, on the other hand, signed the preliminary contract without hesitation. You can be proud that you got what we asked for in the ad. Usually the deals are about twenty percent lower."

Irene thought about it. "Can I still withdraw from the sale?"

"Of course." The broker sounded disgruntled, but remained eagerly polite. "Then you'll have to pay compensation in the amount of the deposit. And, of course, repay the deposit. We would charge you for our expenses, then we will dissolve the contract between us. You can market your flat yourself."

Or keep it, Irene thought. Then she thought about whether she felt like returning to Catalonia alone for a holiday. She would be able to run into Pep at any time and feel ridiculous. How could she get involved with a man she didn't know at all? Who was only looking for a change because his wife was heavily pregnant and therefore indisposed. She almost ended up in bed with him. The kiss on the sofa had demanded a continuation. She would have thrown all her good intentions overboard. Maybe she just wanted to fall in love to distract herself from her grief over Hubert.

The broker cleared his throat.

"No, it's all right. I'll sell the flat for four hundred and eighty thousand." She spoke in a firm voice. "To this gentleman who paid the deposit." She flipped through her calendar. "Tuesday's date would be fine with me."

She could use all the money in the world. Who knows how long Hubert's accounts were frozen? To implement Jasmin's plans for the hotel, every euro counted. She wasn't sure yet whether the vegan breakfast wouldn't scare off guests, but she didn't want to block her daughter's ideas in general.

And then there was the small fortune in the freezer. She had to go to Cambrils again anyway.

She made the appointment and hung up. After a moment's thought, she dialled Suzie's number.

The voicemail came on.

Irene spoke her message on the tape: "I have a problem. Will you accompany me to Catalonia again?"

With Suzie's help, she would manage to see Pep - Josep Folch i Bosch, she improved - one more time, sign her contract and leave immediately. Okay, leave after a long walk on the beach - with Suzie, not with Pep.

She looked out of the window and imagined walking along the beach with bare feet and feeling the small waves against her calves.

CHAPTER FORTY-NINE

THE PLANE SHOOK AGAIN.

Irene looked steadfastly at the back of the seat in front of her, where a paper bag and a laminated sheet with instructions in case of an emergency landing were stuck. She tried to memorise the individual steps.

The stewardess sat down on a free seat diagonally opposite her and fastened her seat belt. The young woman seemed pale around the nose.

The plane dived into a pocket of air. Irene was easily lifted out of her seat, only the seat belt held her back. Her stomach heaved. She swallowed.

Half an hour ago, the pilot had announced turbulence and had given a strong reminder to fasten their seatbelts. The stewardesses had strode down the aisle and checked that everyone had fastened their seatbelts. Now Irene knew why.

Luckily she had only had one coffee at the airport, otherwise she would probably have to use the bag in the next turbulence. No sooner had she finished the thought than the plane bucked again. Because she had booked at short notice, the middle seats above the wings had already been taken. Irene sat in one of the back rows just before the toilets. She knew that the movements of the airbus were most noticeable here. She cursed her frugality. If only she had paid the premium for business class ... but even in the front it would be noticeable that the plane danced through the vastness of the air like a bucking horse.

Hubert had suffered from a fear of flying. That's why he had driven the long distance to Spain by car, even if it cost him working time. "I don't trust those things," he had said, looking at the planes moving in the sky over Hamburg.

Irene had laughed at him, but silently refrained from suggesting holiday destinations that could only be reached by air. Now, as the plane made an unexpected leap forward, she wondered if Hubert had been right. Then she prayed to herself: All statistics proved that flying was the safest form of transport.

What she was experiencing made statistics seem like a sheet of paper full of theoretical calculations. The forces of nature were stronger than man-made technology. Why had Suzie not come along? She would make bad jokes, hand out chocolate as a cure for everything and, above all, hold her hand. But Suzie was taking a certification programme for yoga teachers and had to hold trial class. After all, Suzie had promised to come in time for the notary appointment. At which Irene had to meet Pep - Josep Folch i Bosch, she improved for the hundredth time.

Why had she already flown today? Irene regretted her decision more with every shake of the plane. In a few days, the weather might have calmed down. In a reflex, she had clicked on the cheap last-minute ticket found on the online portal. The prospect of a few days off with walks on the beach in the sun had not mattered, she told herself. She would simply drive to a neighbouring village, to rule out a chance encounter with a man with sea-blue eyes and a pregnant wife, and wander along the beach there.

"We are beginning our approach to Barcelona. Please switch off all electronic devices."

In any case, the tables at the back of the front seats had already been folded up because of the turbulence. The last laptops and tablets had also been put away one by one, because no one could concentrate on a monitor with the violent movements of the plane.

"The weather in Barcelona: eighteen degrees and strong wind. You must have noticed that already."

The pilot could save his sarcasm, Irene thought.

Then he continued: "We will land in about twenty minutes. We wish you a pleasant stay."

Then Irene's ears popped. She held her nose and blew out violently to equalise the pressure, which was only half successful. The plane slumped into an air pocket, then dipped to the left. Irene clung to the armrests.

Next to her sat an Indian woman who consistently slept through all the excitement. She wore an eye mask and noise-cancelling earphones.

Maybe they cancelled everything, Irene thought, determined to buy herself a set. If you could sleep through even heavy turbulence with them, they were worth any price.

In the row in front of her, the toddler she had been flirting with through the gap between the seats at the beginning of the flight began to scream. The mother made soothing 'hsh hsh' sounds, but the child shrieked all the louder. The plane tilted to the other side. Irene caught a glimpse of a wide blue, rippled with white crests. Despite the sinking feeling in her stomach, joy ran through her. The sea! Soon she would be walking along the beach in her bare feet again. If this thing brought her down safely.

At that moment there was a dull sound, a jolt went through the plane. Then the plane sped across the tarmac. Irene watched the concrete runway of the airport whiz by. She uttered a prayer of thanks, loosened her claw grip around the armrest.

"Welcome to Barcelona! Please remain seated with your seatbelts fastened until we have reached the landing position."

The passengers began to clap. Reluctantly, Irene joined in. After all, it was the crew's job to get her here. No one clapped when she had set the breakfast tables correctly. But given the fierce wind, the landing was probably worth applauding. Whatever was waiting for her in Cambrils, it couldn't be worse than this flight, she decided, stood up and dragged her bag out of the hand luggage stowage.

CHAPTER FIFTY

IRENE COULDN'T SLEEP A WINK. Outside, the wind rumbled louder and louder.

The blinds rattled.

Irene rolled over onto her other side and squeezed her eyes tightly shut. She began to count. That usually helped to fall asleep. But not today. She gave up at ninety-seven.

Rhythmically, the waves crashed against the beach. They drowned out the usual background noise. Probably no one was out and about in this weather anyway, there were no car engine noises or human voices to be heard. But the waves were all the clearer.

Would the floodwater overflow the promenade and enter the housing complex? Was the stability of the building at risk?

Irene pushed the thought away. The house had been there for decades and had survived all previous storms.

There was a loud bang. Something had fallen on the balcony. Irene was afraid to pull up the shutter and look. If she opened the shutter, maybe the window would shatter if any more objects flew against it. It was probably just a flowerpot, she told herself, although the bang had been much too loud for that.

She turned back to her other side and pulled the duvet over her ears to hear less of the noise. As soon as she closed her eyes, she remembered the argument she had had with Jasmin. So far, the daughter had not contacted her. No wonder, after the nasty things Irene had said. She really needed to apologise.

Then the hail started. It sounded as if the house had come under fire. Gun salvos pelted against the plastic slats of the shutters. Irene gave up trying to fall asleep. She rolled out of bed, visited the toilet and staggered into the living room. At the kitchen counter, she brewed a cup of tea.

And she had come all the way for the weekend at the beach! She had been looking forward to walks on the strand under a bright blue sky before she got to the bottom of a few things on Monday. Blue skies, no way. It seemed like the end of the world was coming.

She sipped her hot tea carefully. Maybe she could sleep after the storm, spend the whole Sunday in bed. At least Carlos had the door repaired in a makeshift fashion. A chipboard panel had been screwed over the entire door leaf so that the break-in marks were no longer visible. If she just stayed in bed, no one would notice her presence, no one would disturb her.

It was banging again. Objects seemed to be polka dancing on her balcony.

Irene opened the fridge. Yawning emptiness stared back at her. As soon as she arrived, she had checked to see if the money was still there. She was relieved to find the spinach packet in the freezer untouched. It wasn't her money, to be sure, and besides, she thought it was dubious to have so much cash in the house. But in the meantime, she had decided to see it as a small compensation for all the terrible knowledge she had learned about Hubert.

On Wednesday, right after the notary appointment, her flight went back to Hamburg, then she would take the money with her. The large sum should actually be declared to customs, but since she had no idea where the notes came from, she would avoid that. She trusted her harmless appearance and the rush of passengers. It was unlikely that she, of all people, would be waved out for a spot check. If she could manage to look innocent, she told herself. She would think about that when the time came.

The tea had gone cold.

Irene groped into the bedroom, lay down in bed, pulled the covers over herself and hoped to find sleep on the second attempt while the storm raged on outside. She listened to the rattling of the blinds.

Sleep must have overtaken her at some point, because she woke up and it was quiet. She lay there for a while, massaged her aching shoulder, wiggled her toes to get her circulation going, and finally got up. When she pulled up the roller shutter, she saw the mess on the balcony.

Flower pots from an upper floor lay smashed on the floor. The plastic chairs had slid to one side. Something white was lying in one corner. Irene opened the door and looked curiously. They were hailstones the size of pigeon eggs.

Whitecaps could be seen on the sea, otherwise it looked innocent. Nothing remained of the breakers that had crashed onto the beach at night.

CHAPTER FIFTY-ONE

IRENE LOOKED at the beach promenade in shock: it was covered with sand, mud and flotsam. Huge puddles, more like pools of water, lay on the road. She carefully circled a puddle. A bent palm tree lay on the beach, its stump stretched accusingly towards the sky. Some paving slabs had been pushed up and shifted. A car parked in front of the apartment complex had dents on the roof. Irene thought of the hailstones on her balcony. They had certainly caused the pattering that had sounded like a rifle volley.

Now there was no wind. The sun shone innocently. The parakeets in the palm trees were shouting messages to each other as usual. Irene walked along the promenade, repeatedly dodging washed-up branches and pools of water. Workers in bright yellow jackets had connected hoses to hydrants and were flushing mud into the drains in semi-circular movements.

At the harbour, the boats were lined up as usual, but one of the smaller ones was floating upside down between them. She imagined their anchors must have been torn loose. When she arrived at the café, she realised that the idea of having breakfast here in peace had been naïve. All the chairs and tables had been moved aside. Carlos had a shovel in his hand and was shovelling out mud. Juan followed him with a broom and cleaned the area Carlos had cleared. Neighbours, some of whom Irene knew by sight, were busy cleaning on the other side of the room.

The owner of the café collected broken glass in a rubbish bag.

The television was on in the background with a Catalan channel. Irene didn't understand the words, but there was a ticker tape with the latest news. From the written Catalan she recognised a few terms. There was talk of three deaths and two and a half thousand emergency calls last night. Images of fallen trees, unleashed inland rivers and floods flickered across the screen.

The café owner was fidgeting with the remote control. Now he switched on a Spanish channel. An announcer with a serious face reported that the farmers in the Ebro Delta feared losses of the rice harvest, because about three thousand hectares of cultivated land had been flooded with salt water. Then a spokesperson for the Ministry of the Environment was interviewed. Irene didn't get all of it, but basically it was about the beaches on Spain's eight thousand kilometres of coastline. Their fine sandy beaches were at risk from flooding.

Pictures of damaged embankments were shown. The ministry's press spokesperson spoke about the increasing construction, the regulation of rivers and reservoirs. Not enough sediment is being washed down the rivers to the beaches anymore. Climate change makes it more likely that storms like the one at the weekend will increase, he said. In the past three years, this destructive so-called temporal has occurred every year, more frequently than in previous decades.

Spain pays ten million euros a year to replenish the beaches with sand, knowing full well that this too will be eroded by the sea, the TV spokesperson continued. Irene thought of the wonderful feeling of the fine grains of sand between her toes. That's what made a beach walk so special, apart from the sea of course. A beach without sand, what would that be? The prospect terrified her.

Then she shook off the sad thoughts, grabbed a broom and energetically helped to clean the café. After a few hours, everything was back in place. The owner provided all the helpers with coffee, gave Irene a beaming smile and thanked her profusely. He seemed to feel uneasy that the tourist had also lent a hand. This was apparently expected by the neighbours. A woman came by with a tray in her hand, covered with a tea towel. Underneath was a juicy tortilla, which she distributed to everyone present.

After the snack, everyone got back to work, but the worst was already done. Irene wiped down the tables.

Suddenly she heard a familiar voice behind her.

"Hello!"

She turned around.

Pep smiled warmly at her.

A stab went through her heart. She turned away and went to another table.

Pep followed her. "Irene, let's talk."

He just wants to ease his conscience, she thought. He could enjoy himself with her, take a little time out from the wife, who certainly suffered from emotional fluctuations in her heavily pregnant state. I've no desire to sleep with him, she thought bitterly.

Pep persisted.

"I can explain everything to you."

"Damn it, leave me alone!"

CHAPTER FIFTY-TWO

HE WATCHED as Irene energetically pushed the broom over the mud-covered floor, with a powerful swing, again and again. Since he was standing behind a pillar of the balustrade, she had not yet spotted him.

The storm had caused terrible destruction. He had never experienced anything like it. The river raged along its bed muddy brown, lucky that it had not burst its banks. Inland, rivulets had turned into raging torrents, trees had been uprooted and dragged along, bridges had been destroyed, entire houses had collapsed. They had been lucky here on the coast.

All the neighbours were busy cleaning up, and he also helped where he could. The German woman, however, did not have to help, after all, she did not live here. Nevertheless, she helped out. Now Carlos smiled encouragingly at her.

Did he want something from her? Jealousy flashed through Pep's mind. Carlos was a real German, even if he had been living here for decades. Full-blooded German, unlike him, who lived between worlds and didn't really belong anywhere. Perhaps the two had discovered common ground. Besides, Carlos had another unfair advantage: he was Irene's neighbour. Under some pretext, he would always be able to visit Irene. Pep considered whether he could knock Carlos down without further ado. Then he pushed the thought away. Strange, he had never been so possessive with Ana. That's why she had met a boy in Barcelona, a nasty inner voice sneered.

Irene wiped a strand of hair from her forehead. He would have liked to step up to her and brush back her curls himself. Why had Ana unexpectedly burst into their rendezvous the other day? It wasn't as if he had wanted to keep her existence a secret. He would just have liked to explain his situation to Irene little by little.

He swallowed. If he was honest with himself, he had shied away from describing his complicated phase in life. Would Irene have believed him that he was separated from Ana when they were living together under the same roof? At least he had sorted that out now, his ex had moved out. She had taken her things out of the bathroom, he had noticed. She should be happy in Barcelona!

Why was Irene actually here already? He had expected her to arrive shortly before the notary appointment and to leave soon afterwards. He would use the appointment to talk things over with her. But now she had unexpectedly arrived earlier, that gave him the opportunity to excuse himself and perhaps spend some time with her. He gave himself a jolt and walked towards Irene. She was wiping the tables with a cloth.

He leaned forward. "Hello!"

She turned around, her eyes widening. Then she turned away, went to another table.

Pep followed her. "Irene, let's talk."

She had to hear him out. Had she forgotten how close they had become? How good it had felt to be together?

"I can explain everything to you."

"Damn it, leave me alone!" Her voice sounded harsh.

That brought him to his senses. Maybe she needed time? Or should he write her a letter to explain everything calmly? In the old-fashioned way, he could reach for paper and pen.

Pep left the café and walked along the promenade, carefully skirting the pools of water so as not to expose his suede loafers to moisture and dirt. Then he found himself in front of his sister's house. The dog ran towards him barking loudly. When Fosca recognised him, she jumped joyfully around his legs. Pep bent down and stroked her.

Montse was sitting on the balcony and had spread out the accessories for her silver jewellery on the table. With a small pair of pliers, she bent the silver wire into intricate figures. In the summer she sold the stuff to tourists and earned enough to live on for the year, albeit at a low level. She had refused all his offers to finance an education for her.

He greeted his sister with kisses on the cheek.

"Coffee is in the kitchen!"

He fetched two cups and also put a small pot with milk in it. Returned to the balcony.

"Did you get through the storm okay?"

He nodded. They told each other what they had experienced the previous night. Then Pep lapsed into silence.

Montse drank her coffee, threading coloured glass beads onto a wire between each sip. "What's on your mind?"

The sister always sensed when something was wrong. With a sigh, Pep told how Irene had rejected him. Damn it, she could at least have listened to him. Did he have to go after her?

"You've thoroughly blown it," Montse summed up. "What are you going to do now?"

If he only knew. He played around with a piece of wire she had snipped off. "She can stay away from me," he finally said.

"Just like that?" Montse raised her eyebrows.

CHAPTER FIFTY-THREE

THE WEEK BEGAN with glorious sunshine. The sea lay flat as a sheet, looking innocent. People had hurriedly cleaned up the mud and dirt, but it would still take time to remove the worst of the damage. On the beach, a dredger was busy collecting the fallen palm tree and heavy flotsam.

Irene blinked into the light. It blinded her. She had come a few days earlier because of the warmth and the sun. Now she didn't really understand why she had come so urgently before the notary appointment. Certainly not because of a man with sea-blue eyes. She didn't want to run into him. But now Pep had met her without her being able to avoid him. Had he come to the café especially for her?

She pushed the thought aside, got into the rental car and drove to Salou. The place was busier than Cambrils. Although it was still low season, there were clearly more tourists walking around than in the neighbouring town. One long street was completely lined with junk shops selling inflatable swimming aids with animals of all kinds, cheap sunglasses and swimwear in garish colours. A huge plastic flamingo crowned one of the kiosks. Irene's eyes ached at the sight of the merchandise.

She drove to the address of the hotel Hubert had been involved in building. The sat nav led her to a road that wound its way up a mountain. The street signs indicated *Cap de Salou.* Here were larger villas and modern houses with architectural pretensions. No junk in pseudo-Hispanic style. No decoration from the DIY store in the front gardens.

Finally, the sat nav said in its artificial voice, "You have reached your destination." She parked by the side of the road more poorly than she could manage, got out and examined the car. Unless a truck was passing, she would not obstruct the traffic.

Then she turned around and was taken by the view. Wow! From up here she could see the sea on both sides of the cape. Far on the horizon, container ships were pushing their way towards Tarragona. Closer to the coast, a few sailing yachts bobbed on the water. Surfers were visible off the long beach of Salou, their sails white triangles against the dark blue. Seagulls hovered above Irene's head, so adept at exploiting air currents that sometimes they almost stood still in one place, then glided elegantly away again without a flap of their wings.

Irene tore herself away from the picturesque sight and looked at the construction site with the hotel complex. For it still looked like a building site. What would later become green spaces was still bare earth. Steel girders lay next to the road, pallets with paving stones piled up next to them. Just in front of Irene stood a larger building with a curved driveway, the prominent entrance flanked by two columns. Further back, several smaller houses nestled against the flank of the hill. Apparently, each one had a sea view.

She looked over her shoulder. Far and wide there was no one to be seen.

Irene went up the stairs of the central building and rattled the door. Locked. She peered through the window. There was no furniture, but everything else seemed finished. The walls were painted white, a ceiling lamp was installed.

Then she felt a pair of eyes on her. Perceived a movement in the room.

A huge black dog with pointed ears sat under the window and looked up at her. His tail was thumping on the floor, that was the movement she had sensed. Irene almost choked with fright. Was this a Doberman? Fortunately, he was not running free on the grounds.

Irene pulled back from the window, went down the stairs and rounded a few puddles on her way to the nearest smaller house. Looked around again to make sure her car was not obstructing traffic. That did not seem to be the case. In any case, the street was uncrowded.

A man in dark clothes was standing next to a bush, leaning over a bit. He was obviously taking a piss. Surely a security guard, it flashed through Irene's mind. To take a leak, he had chosen a corner that was not visible from the street.

But since she had already entered the compound, there was no point in going back and possibly drawing his attention.

She approached the smaller building, right next to the entrance there was apparently a terrace, a wooden substructure had already been installed. Irene stepped between the planks, carefully placing her feet so as not to slip or get stuck. She put her hands to the window and shaded the pane to look through. This was apparently a large living room with a kitchenette. Cables hung out of the wall in the corner, a power strip was already installed.

Apparently, a complex was planned that combined the best of a hotel and a holiday home. Irene imagined what it would be like to run such a facility up here on the headland. She would provide breakfast for the guests and offer an optional dinner in the main house. But the kitchenette also made it possible to prepare a little something yourself. Residents could choose whether they wanted to be looked after or preferred to cater for themselves. An idea of modern hospitality that Irene had flirted with for a long time. I wonder if Hubert had put her suggestions into practice here? Without talking to her about it?

She tore herself away from the sight of the half-finished interior, trudged further up the slope and repeated her manoeuvre at the next house. Here, little more than the shell stood. The walls were not plastered, electrical wiring not yet laid.

"Hey, what are you doing?"

Irene flinched and turned around.

The man dressed in black approached her. There was some kind of logo emblazoned on the breast pocket of his jacket. The guard was of short, broad build, had pitch-black short hair and a bronze complexion. The large black dog she had seen through the window earlier was at his side, tugging excitedly at the leash, panting. "Privado! This is private property." With a gesture, the man circumscribed the whole area.

"I just wanted to look around." Irene smiled kindly at him.

The dog tugged harder, so the man dug his heels into the ground to hold him. "Vayase! There's nothing to look at here."

"It's okay, I'm going." Irene kept away from the dog, walked in a semicircle around him and the man and slowly returned to her car. She realised that she had penetrated several hundred metres into the hotel complex and now had to go back a correspondingly long way. Frighteningly far, considering the dog. If it barked, she would feel safer, but the critter just kept panting.

The man followed her on her heels.

Irene half turned as she walked slowly on. She felt uneasy about being alone with the man. There was still traffic on the street. If at first she had feared obstructing buses or trucks with the parked car, now she wished there were more cars down there. Someone would be watching what was happening here.

"I just wanted to see if you could buy one of the houses. Who do I have to contact if I want to be here?" She tried to look like a harmless tourist with lots of money. She babbled on. "The view is so great, if I imagine vacationing here …. is this maybe a timeshare model?"

"Not for sale." The man waved his hands as if he could get rid of them faster that way.

Irene circled back around the puddles that the storm had left behind here as well, reached the gate and used the remote control to pop open the car door.

The guard stopped at the entrance to the compound with his dog. He had done his job.

Irene got in, started the engine and frantically accelerated. The engine choked and died.

Hectically, she turned the key back to the left and started again. This time it worked.

She gave the guard one last look. The dog had sat down next to him and let his long, red tongue hang out.

The man had taken out his mobile phone, now pointed it at Irene's car and took a photo.

Irene stepped violently on the gas, the car lurched forward, then she got it under control and hurriedly drove back the way she had come. As she lurched through bends, she wondered if the man would report her intrusion to anyone. Strange that he had taken a photo. Only because a curious tourist had inspected the grounds. The rental car cannot be traced back to me, even if you know the car number, she reassured herself. It had no sticker or label from the rental company.

CHAPTER FIFTY-FOUR

THE OLD TOWN of Cambrils was remarkably picturesque. Anyone who had only explored the beach promenade with its modern buildings would never have guessed that such a gem was hidden a few streets away. Irene marvelled at the narrow alleys of small houses more than a hundred years old. Some alleys were completely filled with flower pots full of green plants, so that you couldn't even get through them with a moped. Somehow, she had overlooked this part of the town until now.

The address Irene had photographed from the building plans was located in a backyard down one of the alleys. A metal sculpture stood on a manicured lawn. Through a glass door, Irene entered a stairwell and went up to the first floor. Next to the door of the shared office hung a whole lath of company signs, including one for Gonzalez S.A. It was a co-working space, she realised.

She rang the bell and immediately a buzzing sound indicated the door had opened. She pushed it open and came into a bright room with a reception desk where a young woman with dark brown hair sat. The large room also contained a table tennis table and a kind of bar with a large professional coffee machine. In one corner, a couple of young people sat on uncomfortable-looking stools. They were bent over a laptop that stood on a cube of orange felt. They were discussing quietly but animatedly. On a beanbag chair by the window, a man lounged with speakers over his ears, typing on his mobile phone.

In the background, soft bagpipe music was playing, which reminded Irene strongly of the Indian sound sequences that Suzie used for her yoga classes.

Irene turned to the woman at the reception desk. "Buenos días, I'm looking for Manuel Martines."

"Who?"

She repeated the name.

"Don't know it."

Irene pulled out her mobile phone and checked the photo of the address from Hubert's documents.

"Manuel Martines of Gonzalez S.A."

"Oh him. I'm sorry, Senor Martines is not here."

"When can I meet him?"

"Do you have an appointment?"

"Unfortunately, no, I dropped in spontaneously."

"Please contact him by email and you can make an appointment."

"I thought this was where his business was based?"

"That's right." The young woman tossed her hair back. "We are a co-working space. There are a lot of start-ups here and also established companies like Gonzalez S.A. But many employees work remotely and rarely come by."

Irene frowned. The working world was becoming more and more confusing. Were construction projects managed from home offices? Didn't they need lots of technical draughtsmen, accountants or at least assistants?

As if she could read minds, the dark-haired woman said, "I am the virtual assistant of these companies." She pointed to the shelf behind her, which was divided into many low compartments containing letters. "These are their mailboxes. I handle the communications. Once a week or at your convenience, the owners come and get their mail. Make an appointment with Senor Martines and you can meet him here."

A letterbox company? Things were getting more and more opaque. Irene thanked him politely and left.

As soon as she was on the street, her phone rang. It was Jasmin calling.

Irene greeted her warmly.

Jasmin sounded excited. She was doing well, she said, and she now had an idea of how she could make the transition to a climate-friendly hotel without waiting for the inheritance to be released. "Leon put me up to it." She huffed out the words as if afraid Irene would interrupt her. "You can take out a loan on crowdfunding."

"Crowd... what?"

"Crowdfunding. These are platforms where private people grant loans at very favourable interest rates. You just have to explain your project and inspire as many people as possible.

Irene secretly cursed the day Jasmin had met this Leon. Jasmin was already talking.

"By the way, do you know what happened to Pops' Bitcoin wallets? Did the police even discover them? Maybe there's still money on there."

"You knew about the Bitcoins?"

"Sure, he was super proud about it."

Irene bit her lip. Hubert seemed to have shared more information with her daughter than with her.

"I didn't know anything about it, but the police have their eyes on the wallets." Kroeger had said something about it, she remembered. "Do you know anything else I don't?"

"Oh, Mum, you were always at the hotel. You hardly ever saw each other.

"The hotel has helped us to afford our standard of living." Irene realised that her words sounded more biting than intended. Still, she couldn't help adding, "And you want to ruin it with your rabbit food breakfast." She hung up.

Staring at the mobile phone. What had she done now?

CHAPTER FIFTY-FIVE

"WELL, do you want to join us?" Xavi grinned at him.

"Oh no, thanks." Inwardly, Pep shuddered to imagine other people crawling up his body. He was happy to acknowledge the Castellers' achievement, but for him a sport with that much physical contact was not suitable. Xavi knew that very well and just wanted to tease him a little.

Pep patted him on the back. He spent the next half hour watching the Colla train. He had nothing better to do and the tension kept him from worrying. About Irene, for instance. Or about his wife, whom he would divorce as soon as possible.

Now the Colla had built up a so-called Pillar, the figure of a pillar with six people standing on top of each other. The man on the third floor lost his balance. He swayed, and already the whole tower was collapsing. The Castellers deftly dropped and were caught by their comrades without anyone getting hurt. At the annual competition, which always took place in Tarragona, such a demolition would of course not have earned any points. But for the Colla, the fun of their sport was paramount.

Xavi thanked all the participants, then they began to say goodbye. Sashes were rolled up, sweaty shirts changed, bags packed.

Xavi pulled Pep aside to escape the general confusion. He handed his friend a can of lemonade and tore one open himself.

They drank, Xavi clearly being more thirsty. "Well, how's it going with the tourist?" the Cap de Colla asked, when he had set the can down.

He squeezed the can in his fist.

"Not so good right now." Pep didn't feel like talking about their encounter. How she had given him the cold shoulder. To change the subject, he told him about his research into the hotel complex in Salou.

Xavi didn't bat an eyelid when he heard about the prices of the construction project. Here on the coast, people were used to speculation.

"The Colombians have to make a good cut now if this is to pay off."

Pep took another sip of iced lemonade.

"Colombian?" Xavi listened up.

Pep shrugged his shoulders. "Apparently the hotel is now owned by Colombians who are finishing it and then leasing it out. Or run it themselves."

"They won't run it themselves, they'll sell it again. It's all about money laundering."

"You think so?"

"Sure, it's the drug mafia that has to invest its money somehow. You have no idea what sums are in circulation."

Xavi explained. "The peace process in Colombia has given the drug mafia time and peace to establish itself in Europe. The Latin American country produces more than a thousand tonnes of cocaine annually. The gateway to Europe, where the prices for the illegal goods are much higher than in the country of origin and also than in the USA, is Algeciras on the Gibraltar Channel. Kapos have settled there in luxury villas, the area is known as 'Little Medellín'. The large port of Tarragona is a second port of call, and in the hinterland, laboratories for processing coca paste have already been busted. The buyers are Russians, Albanians, Turks ... a total of eight nationalities are known to buy the imported goods from the Colombian clans. You can't imagine the sums of money involved. The capos drive Jaguars, send their children to elite schools and buy dozens of properties in a short time."

If Xavi said that, it had to be true, because his father was in the Mossos, the Catalan police. Pep took his word for it.

"Who knows if the German knew about it."

"If he got involved in deals with the Colombians, he was either naïve or involved."

Pep scratched his head. It was none of his business. Hubert Hansen should rest in peace and, after all, he had nothing to do with Irene. Still, "I'd like to know what went on." The words had slipped out of his mouth.

"Don't interfere!"

"Why?"

"The Colombians are dangerous. Really dangerous. They don't hesitate if someone gets in their way. There are rumours of disappearances, of outright executions."

"In the middle of Europe? Here in Spain?"

Xavi pursed his lips. Then he said: "Back in the eighties, mercenaries for the drug mafia were trained here in Galicia. Former Israeli officers led the training in the camp. The graduates were then a private troop of kapos. Officially, they were registered as a security force. Since then, conditions have not improved. The kapos have armed troops with military training. In short, stay away from them, that's all I can say."

CHAPTER FIFTY-SIX

THE ATMOSPHERE in the office was icy.

The notary cleared his throat. He too seemed to notice that something was wrong. He looked from one to the other, no one returned his gaze. Irene stared at the tabletop. Pep eyed the framed certificates and awards on the wall.

The notary began with a flowery statement in which he emphasised that he represented the Spanish state and testified that the planned real estate deal was legal. He read out the names and addresses of the parties involved, then quoted the name of Irene's flat in the land register. Her name was not mentioned, the selling part was Daurada Ltda.'.

Irene looked up briefly, only to see that Pep was staring out of the window inquisitively. His big strong fingers were playing with a pen. She quickly returned her gaze to the table. Next to her, the broker moved uneasily in his chair. The notary now emphasised the agreed purchase sum and pointed out the existing preliminary contract.

Irene suddenly realised that she would never again drink her morning coffee sitting on the terrace with a view of the sea. If I want that, I'll just go to a hotel, she thought defiantly. Still, it was a pity that the flat now went to Pep, who was rich anyway, considering the dimensions of his villa. He would now be able to rent out the flat to tourists at exorbitant prices and put away a pretty penny, she thought bitterly.

On the other hand, it was good to part with the flat. It would have reminded her forever and ever of Hubert's betrayal, plus the fiasco with Pep. No, she wanted to get rid of the flat, she was sure of that. Hamburg was a nice place to live and if she wanted sun, she could always book a holiday in the south. Let Pep fix up the flat and leave it to tourists. She didn't care, she told herself.

The notary read out the text of the purchase contract in a professionally practised singsong. The translator, whom Irene had hired for safety's sake, repeated sentence after sentence in German. On the return flight tomorrow, Irene would be a lot richer. The proceeds from the flat would go into her own account, the police couldn't freeze that. She could finally realise her wishes to bring the hotel up to date. Still, she felt no joy. She could still sleep one last night in the flat, listen to the surf at night.

Then the notary finished and pushed the contract towards her. She hesitated for a moment, then she signed it with a flourish. Maybe Jasmin and Leon's ideas were not so bad. The young generation addressed the ideas of tomorrow's tourists. She thanked the notary and translator, put her documents in her handbag and stood up. Went to the door. Suddenly Pep was standing next to her. She had been avoiding his gaze the whole time.

"If I may tell you something." Pep took a deep breath. "Hubert and the Colombians ..."

"No, you mustn't," Irene snapped at him. Immediately she was startled by her harsh reaction. She reached out to Pep, but he had already turned around. She could just see him purse his lips together.

Suzie was waiting for her outside the door and fell around her neck. "Everything went well?" she trumpeted.

She nodded. Her friend had flown here especially to make the sale easier for her. That touched her. Now they would relax for a few days and then return to Hamburg. Irene could forget about this love nest on the Mediterranean and get back to her daily worries about the hotel.

Her next goal was to increase the occupancy rate so that it would become profitable again. Whether Jasmin's way was the right one, she doubted. Who wanted to have substitute scrambled eggs for breakfast?

As if Suzie had read her mind, she suggested going out to eat. "The sale must be celebrated!"

CHAPTER FIFTY-SEVEN

Suzie dabbed yellow-green olive oil from her plate with the bread. She leaned back and rubbed her belly. "Oh man, that was delicious!"

Irene had suggested visiting one of the classy fish restaurants on the seafront. "I'll pay!" After all, she had just taken in a huge chunk of money. She could throw her usual thriftiness overboard for once and treat herself to a restaurant visit with her friend. Suzie was immediately enthusiastic, as always when it came to food.

"Now you're rid of the flat," Suzie said.

She waved at the waiter. When the waiter approached the table, she asked for the dessert menu.

"Next holiday in the Caribbean!"

Irene wondered if she wanted to go there at all. She tried to sense whether she was relieved about the sale of the flat.

"Or to the North Sea," Suzie added when she noticed her friend's restrained reaction. "The main thing is that you can forget Hubert's misstep now."

If it were that simple, Irene thought. Over thirty years of marriage and then everything forgotten? Hubert's inheritance included not only the flat, but also a pile of cash of unknown origin, a mistress, drug traces in the car, prepaid mobile phones and involvement in a construction scandal. Because if she was honest with herself, something was wrong with the construction site of the hotel complex in Salou. Why weren't the houses finished? Why did the construction company lodge in a co-working space so that it resembled a letterbox company? Questions upon questions.

"Can you imagine Hubert getting paid in cash?"

Now it was out. Irene pressed her lips together.

Suzie lifted her head from the card. "The architectural firm VHB collects illegal cash payments? Hardly. What makes you think that?"

"The cash Hubert left behind. It has to come from somewhere."

"VHB has existed since the beginnings of the Federal Republic, it is a Hanseatic institution. They don't need that."

Irene raised her shoulders. Dropped them again. Said nothing. Maybe Hubert had collected on his own account, it had nothing to do with the VHB office. She remembered what Pep had said. That in Spain many properties were sublet and parts of the purchase price were paid in cash. However, Pep had offered her no such arrangement for the flat. She didn't want to think about whether he lacked trust in her. Or whether he wanted to have as little to do with her as possible and settle everything by bank transfer.

Irene's thoughts wandered. She forced herself to follow Hubert's train of thought. If the buyer ... Carlos had mentioned something like that once, in an aside, probably to impress her when she had cleaned up after the Temporal. And she had thought it was nonsense. She hadn't said anything, she'd just thought he should keep his mouth shut and do his yoga exercises. Carlos had suggested that Colombian drug traffickers laundered their drug money with such purchases and sales of real estate. What did Carlos know? But he knew a lot of people. And yes, it was about drugs, in Hubert's car. His murder was one that could be attributed to drug cartels. Inspector Kroeger in Hamburg probably suspected that, too, with his inquiries. There were the Latinos, there were the burglaries. Maybe Carlos wasn't so wrong after all.

So, if some drug cartel bought the half-finished complex from Hubert and offered parts in cash, would he have gone for it? She remembered Hubert's vanity. He had always liked to show off what he owned. That had also been one of the reasons why no investments were possible for the hotel. What Hubert earned, he immediately spent again. Brand-name clothes, the Porsche ... a stack of notes might have tempted him to cheat his own office and fork out on something for himself.

Because the hotel complex in Salou had not been completed, VHB saved itself the complicated cooperation with a dozen trades that were responsible for the interior fittings. It was much easier to erect the shells than to be responsible for the dry construction. In addition, Hubert had the chance to present the securitised, lower purchase price as realistic to his colleagues. After all, the value of the hotel could only be realised when the complex was completed to such an extent that guests could move in.

She told Suzie about the hotel complex and her research.

"Are you crazy? If there are crooked things going on, it's totally dangerous to go snooping around."

Suzie widened her eyes and waved her hands to illustrate how dangerous it was. Irene shook her head. Finding herself alone with the guard and his dog had been unpleasant, but in the end nothing had happened. But she would not let up until she had found out what had driven Hubert to his death. Was he himself responsible for falling victim to a crime? What kind of people had he got involved with? Suzie was on the culinary road again.

"Would you fancy a crema catalana?"

"Why not?"

Irene didn't care what they ate for dessert. But when the little clay bowls with the cream were served and the scent of caramel rose to her nose, she sighed contentedly. The two friends smashed the caramelised sugar layer on the cream and then spooned the sweet pudding with relish.

"Listen!" Suzie avoided her gaze and scratched around in her already empty clay bowl. "I have a date with Carlos."

Irene stared at her. A suspicion sprang up in her mind. Had Suzie arrived to flirt with her neighbour? To tie herself in knots with him in yoga positions? And not to give her moral support in the matter of selling a flat and going out with Pep?

"When?", she managed.

"Right now." Suzie glanced after a young, muscular man who glided past on a skateboard. "Do you want to come?"

"Got plans," Irene said. It sounded more venomous than intended. Was she jealous?

CHAPTER FIFTY-EIGHT

THEY PARTED, Suzie went to Carlos, and Irene set out at a brisk pace to visit the coworking space again. She wanted to ask some of the co-workers what kind of guy this Manuel Martines was. As she walked, she pulled out her mobile phone and called Manfred van Vreeden. After a few words of greeting, she summoned up all her courage and asked: "It's about the hotel complex in Salou. Do you think that part of the purchase price was paid in cash?"

She heard van Vreeden draw in his breath sharply.

"That would be illegal. It violates our Code of Conduct and is not in line with our vision."

Meanwhile, she had reached the roundabout that divided the beach promenade and was the junction with the marina. She briefly checked the traffic before changing sides of the road.

Then she added: "But it would be possible? In Spain, this practice is said to be widespread."

"If it was, it was entirely Hubert's business." Van Vreeden sounded irritated. "I don't know where you get that idea. The VHB office certainly ..."

Tyres squealed next to her.

Startled, she took the mobile phone from her ear and looked up. A white van slammed on its brakes right next to her. With a rolling sound, the back door opened. Two men jumped out. They were wearing dark motorbike masks. Fingers dug into her upper arms. Hands grabbed her. She wriggled and kicked her feet. Hit one of the men in the leg. The other one wrapped his arms around her from behind. Dragged her into the van. Her wriggling did not help. She was thrown roughly onto a seat. Then everything happened very quickly.

It became dark. She felt scratchy tissue on her face. She thought she was suffocating and breathed frantically. This made her breathe even less. She panted in panic. Someone slapped her heartily on the back. She gasped for air, then forced herself to breathe in and out regularly. Her mobile phone was forced out of her hand. Plastic cuffs closed around her wrists so that they were tied in front of her stomach. She screamed, but at that moment the door of the car was closed, she heard the door roll and the lock snap shut.

She felt people sitting to her right and left. It must be the two men who had just jumped out of the van. She felt one of them put the seatbelt around her, straight over her cuffed hands, and snap the buckle. The car started up with a jerk. Irene was pressed into the seat. She screamed, but the bag over her head muffled her voice. The fabric settled on her mouth and nose so that she could no longer breathe. She struggled for breath again, fell silent. The car took a bend, apparently leaving the roundabout.

The whole thing didn't take a minute. Only now did Irene have time to panic. Her stomach cramped, her heart hammered as if it wanted to jump out of her chest .She forced herself to think about breathing. Breathe in, breathe out. Apart from the sound of the engine, nothing could be heard. The car stopped, waited, started again. Apparently, a traffic light. It continued at a moderate pace. Irene tried to count the traffic light stops, but the panic kept confusing her.

Breathe in, breathe out. She thought of the few hours she had spent practising yoga with Suzie. Deep breath in, slow breath out. Her heart calmed a little. The sack smelled of damp and mould. She felt sick. She swallowed hard to keep from vomiting. A gagging sound escaped her.

"Callate," hissed the man on her right. "Silence!"

She concentrated on breathing again. Breathe in, breathe out. After a while, she lost track of time. The car seemed to have reached an motorway, because now it no longer stopped.

CHAPTER FIFTY-NINE

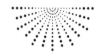

SHE WAS DEAD.

Her shoulder ached.

Wait a minute, weren't dead people relieved of suffering?

It was dark. Nothing to see, nothing to hear.

She rolled onto her side. She found that she was lying on a thin mattress covered with a sheet. Her head was pounding. Her eyes were glued shut. It took effort to open her eyelids. Even that did not make it bright. Was she blind? She straightened up.

There was a glimmer of light. Not dead, not blind, then.

Relief flashed through her.

Still, something was wrong. Where was she?

Then it all came back to her.

The men, the van, the bag over the head.

She sank back, closed her eyes again and curled up. She stayed like that for a while. A few minutes or an hour, she couldn't say.

Cautiously, she opened her eyes again. Nothing had changed. Or had it? The glimmer of light had become brighter, the room was in twilight.

She straightened up. She felt dizzy. She put her head between her knees and waited until she felt better. Then, very slowly, she straightened up again and looked at her surroundings.

She was wearing her clothes, the bag was gone. She ran her fingers over her wrists. The places where the cable ties had cut into them hurt slightly. She was sitting on a double bed in a bedroom. There was a small table, a stool and a wardrobe. A window, but it was somehow darkened. And a door. Irene stood up, still feeling dizzy. She swayed, held onto the wall and felt her way to the door. Opened it.

A tiny bathroom, windowless. Automatically, her hand went to the light switch. The bright light blinded her. She squinted her eyes again. Then she used the toilet, washed her face afterwards. On the shelf was a cup with toothpaste and a toothbrush, still wrapped in plastic. She brushed her teeth, rinsed. There were white hotel-quality towels, she noted unconsciously. Wait, she was in a hotel, wasn't she?

The bathroom was no different from countless similar rooms she had experienced in hotels. Professionally furnished, the space was optimally utilised. The shower looked tempting. But what if she was standing in the shower and someone came in? This was definitely not a holiday. She had weak knees, a bad taste in her mouth and a headache. The kidnappers - they must have been kidnappers - had apparently given her an anaesthetic.

She went back into the room where she had been sleeping. Now she discovered a light switch here too and flicked it on. The bedroom also looked like any other hotel room, apart from the darkened window. There was no cheap art print on the wall either, nothing was furnished at all except for the furniture. She stepped to the window. Curtains were also missing. The window was boarded up on the outside. Between two boards she discovered a slightly larger gap through which light fell.

She tried to peer through the gap, but the light blinded her.

She shook the handle. In vain. The window would not open. She noticed that the frame was screwed tight. Several large screws were driven into it in an irregular pattern.

Irene felt sick to her stomach. She shuffled to the bed, sat down and curled up. This was definitely a kidnapping. They had prepared the room here. Then she heard footsteps, a cough and the door opened.

CHAPTER SIXTY

THE RINGING of the telephone woke Pep. An unknown number.

"Hello?" he said gruffly.

He had treated himself to a whiskey last night to help him sleep. A double. Or two doubles? His throat felt parched. Fortunately, he was in no hurry. The first appointment at the office was not until eleven o'clock, so he could take it easy. If some idiot didn't call at the crack of dawn.

"This is Karl, that is, Carlos. Irene's neighbour."

"Hello." Pep knew only too well who Carlos was. The man who had been very familiar with Irene while cleaning up after the Temporal. Too familiar, for his taste.

"Is Irene with you?"

"What makes you think that?"

He had screwed that up thoroughly. Irene would not be coming here again, he had to come to terms with that.

"She's not with you?"

The man sounded horrified. He spoke a correct Spanish, but with a strong accent. Pep therefore switched to German and asked, "Why should she be with me?" He didn't understand what Carlos wanted from him. Was the guy jealous? Apparently he hadn't noticed that Irene didn't want to know anything more about Pep. That is, Irene hadn't told her neighbour anything. However, she wasn't very open-hearted anyway, it seemed to him.

Nevertheless, a faint hope stirred in him. Hadn't Irene burned all her bridges yet?

"She's disappeared."

"What do you mean, disappeared?"

Pep was beginning to feel like a parrot. He only ever repeated what Carlos said.

"She wasn't home tonight."

"How do you know?", Pep blurted out. He realised that he sounded aggressive.

"Suzie, so this is Irene's friend. Suzie says Irene didn't come home yesterday and still hasn't this morning. So we thought she might be ..."

"No, she's not here," Pep interrupted him. Fear tightened his throat. Where could Irene be? "Maybe she went back to Germany?" he said aloud.

"But her things are here in the flat."

"Now calm down. What happened yesterday? When did you last see her?" There was certainly a rational, harmless explanation, Pep told himself. Carlos said that Irene and Suzie had gone out to eat together after the notary appointment, in one of the fish restaurants at the marina. Then Suzie had come to Carlos. "Suzie is afraid that Irene was mad at her for dating me. We were just going to ..."

"Then where did Irene go?"

Pep didn't care what they wanted. Irene had disappeared! The words rotated in his head.

"That's what we don't know! She wanted to ask about something in a co-working space. It was about this hotel in Salou that her husband had designed."

What had Irene got herself into? He had overheard that she was worried about what her husband had been involved in. Now she was investigating? What had she stumbled upon? Who had she provoked?

"I'll come by," Pep announced and hung up. Then he immediately dialled again and asked the assistant to cancel all appointments for today.

He prepared a coffee in the vending machine, downed it, threw on a jacket and hurried to the door. Irene needed his help, wherever she was, he sensed.

CHAPTER SIXTY-ONE

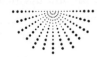

THE DOOR OPENED and a small man with broad shoulders entered. He was wearing jeans and a black T-shirt with *Metallica* written on it. His face was covered by a dark motorbike mask. Irene froze in shock. She stood beside the bed as if rooted to the spot. The man carried a tray, which he placed on the small table. On it was a bottle of water and a baguette topped with something.

Irene relaxed a little. If she got breakfast, he wouldn't kill her. She eyed the man. Was he one of those who had dragged her here yesterday? It was impossible to tell, except that they were all Latino. She had fallen into the hands of a Latino gang. Whatever they wanted from her.

"Eat!" the man said. "We'll talk on the phone later."

"Phone call? With whom?" Maybe the men had got it wrong and thought she was a millionaire's wife or something. "What do you want from me?"

"You came back here like a good girl, otherwise we would have had to follow you to Hamburg."

Okay, there was probably no confusion. The men had it in for her, even wanted to follow her home. She felt cold. Keep the conversation going, she told herself. As long as he was talking to her, he couldn't hit her or harass her. "I don't even know you."

"We'll talk later, eat now!"

He pointed to the tray, turned and left the room. Irene slumped down on the bed. It was a nightmare. An absurd nightmare! Her heart was beating up to her throat. The short exchange of words had exhausted her. She reached for the water bottle and twisted off the cap. It cracked when she opened it, so the bottle had probably not been tampered with. Nevertheless, she sniffed the liquid suspiciously. Then she screwed the bottle back on and decided it was better to drink tap water. Yesterday, the kidnappers had given her a narcotic. It must have been in the water bottle they had put in her hand, as she darkly remembered. After that, she hadn't noticed anything more until she woke up this morning in that hotel room with the barricaded window.

Irene forced herself to breathe slowly and deeply. Her brain was working at full speed. Who were these guys? The man who had brought her breakfast spoke with a Latin accent. Just like the guy who had called her on Hubert's prepaid mobile. Thank you also for your legacy, Hubert. Truly a dangerous legacy you have left me! 'Kidnapped by Latinos'. Sounded like a film title. She giggled frantically. When she became aware of it, she almost choked. Was she going crazy now? Kidnapping mania? Anyway, she would not fall in love with the kidnapper, she firmly resolved. That was a typical reaction, wasn't it? The Stockholm syndrome came to her mind. Useless knowledge.

She would survive this and be free again. She firmly resolved to do that. She bent over the sandwich. It looked harmless. She smelled it. It smelled appetising. She opened it and examined the topping. Cheese, nothing else. No tomato. Definitely not a luxury hotel, she thought bitterly. She bit into the baguette. Only now did she realise how hungry she was. Being kidnapped obviously stimulated the appetite. On the other hand, lunch with Suzie yesterday had been her last meal. Suzie - she would miss her by now. Go to the police and raise the alarm. But Suzie had gone to Carlos. Maybe she was rolling around in bed with him and didn't even notice that Irene had disappeared?

A cold hand clenched around her heart. She had argued with Pep, Suzie was distracted and Jasmin had downright insulted her. No one would miss her, at least not in the next few days. She put the baguette back. She had lost her appetite.

CHAPTER SIXTY-TWO

THE MAN with the Metallica T-shirt pressed a newspaper into her hand. *La Vanguardia* was on the front page.

"Lift!"

She knew these typical blackmail photos from television, but never would she have dreamed of holding such a newspaper up to the camera herself. Images from her childhood flashed in her brain, a washed-out photo of a man with a spongy face, half-hidden behind a newspaper. "Employer President Schleyer ..."

She jerked herself forcibly out of her thoughts.

"Look this way!" the other one ordered her. He had mounted his mobile phone on a tripod, which he now aligned in front of her.

"You say they should pay! And that you're fine."

I'm not well, not at all, she thought defiantly. Her mind was racing. This was her opportunity to deliver a message. But what if they cut the message after the fact? Still, she had to try. They probably didn't understand German anyway. And she would speak German.

The man fiddled with the mobile phone, then growled, "So, Cariño, now recite your line!"

"Hello," Irene began uncertainly. She had no idea who would see her in this state. Who the kidnappers were going to send this video to. Hopefully Suzie would get to see it, she was pragmatic and would know what to do, she tried to reassure herself. She stared at the mobile phone. She must have looked ridiculous. Her hair was a mess. But who cares, the hairstyle doesn't matter now. She gave herself a jolt.

"I'm fine so far. Please help me, do what they say. I want to get out of here. And see if I defrosted the freezer!"

"What is she babbling about?" asked the one with the mobile phone.

The other shrugged his shoulders.

"Habla español!"

She repeated in Spanish what she had said. Instead of the sentence from the freezer, she said, "I'd love to eat spinach with you again. Get me out of here!"

At that moment, loud dog barking started outside. The guard! Would he notice and save her? Irene got out of step. She stuttered out the message in Spanish. Then she remembered that the guard had been Latino, like his kidnappers. Was he in cahoots with the Metallica fan and his accomplices?

Then new hope sprang up in her. Perhaps a stranger was approaching, a policeman even, who wanted to free her? And the dog barked frantically to warn its master of an unknown intruder.

"No police," the Metallica fan hissed at her.

"And no police!" she repeated dutifully.

The kidnapper next to her snatched the newspaper from her hand. "That's enough now."

"She is completely confused. What is she babbling about spinach? Stop it!"

The second man seemed to be the boss. He spoke less. The menial jobs like bringing food for the hostage and directing the mobile phone had to be done by the one with the hardcore T-shirt. Since both were masked and hardly differed in size and shape, Irene had a hard time remembering their appearance. In case she was freed and could make a statement.

Irene hoped that her message had got across. She had no idea what the kidnappers were demanding or from whom, but if it was money, the recipients of the message should at least have a chance of finding the cash in her fridge. Hopefully Suzie was shrewd enough to take the hint. How else was she going to escape this situation?

CHAPTER SIXTY-THREE

IRENE WANDERED up and down the room.

Ten steps there, ten steps back.

The constant artificial light was getting on her nerves. Being shut in depressed her more and more every minute. She missed the wind in her hair and the salty sea air on her skin. She missed hugs and kind words.

She let out a sob. Would she ever be free again?

Her pace quickened. There was no point in despairing. The kidnappers had made their demand. She only hoped Suzie had taken their hint about the spinach packet. At least then the ransom was there. If Suzie was the recipient, which she hoped she was. Would her friends call the police? Would that be a good move or a bad one?

She didn't like to think that Jasmin had been dragged into the matter. But the kidnappers knew nothing of her daughter's existence, and that's how it should stay.

She wanted to kick something, she was so frustrated.

Pacing back and forth did not help her get rid of the restlessness. She forced herself to calm down, leaning against the table. It gave way.

She staggered a step backwards.

The table was obviously very wobbly. She looked at it more closely. The model looked familiar to her. It seemed to come from a Swedish furniture store, which - to Hubert's dismay - she had also visited from time to time. Some of the furniture had been with her since her training and she didn't want to miss it, even if it looked pretty worn out by now.

Irene took a closer look at the table. One of the legs was slightly askew. It had obviously loosened under her weight when she had leaned against it. She bent down and looked under the tabletop.

The legs were screwed to the table top from below and secured with wing nuts. Irene tried turning the screw on the leg, which was already a little crooked. It opened easily. After a few minutes, Irene had dismantled the table leg. She weighed it thoughtfully in her hand.

CHAPTER SIXTY-FOUR

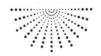

THE SUN WAS JUST RISING above the horizon, the sky glowing golden. Only a few people were out and about. Surely the reason why the kidnappers had chosen this time of day, thought Pep.

An elderly lady was limping around the harbour entrance with a dog of indeterminate breed. The dog sank its snout into a collection of seaweed and dirt. Pep and Carlos looked at each other. They gave each other the thumbs up as a sign that everything would go well. Pep hadn't been thrilled when Carlos had offered to come along, but had agreed, because the two of them could protect Suzie better, and Xavi stayed at home as back-up. Someone had to do something, after all, in case the trio got out of the way today. Pep pushed the thought aside and looked around.

Further back by the harbour master's building stood a man, a stocky guy who wore strangely chunky glasses. Maybe a specialist who repaired the boats with the help of smart glasses? But he wasted no further thought on it. An iron fist clutched his heart. Nothing could happen to Irene!

His gaze rested on Suzie's petite figure as she stepped through the port gate onto the pier. After a few steps, she had left the building with the port administration and the restaurant 'Confraria del Port' behind her. The pier was now exposed to the wind, which blew weakly but steadily. Waves slapped rhythmically against the boulders at the foot of the breakwater.

Suzie impatiently brushed her hair behind her ear. The red backpack on her back shone in the morning light. A handbag would have sufficed for the ransom, but Suzie was the sporty type and didn't own one. Two hundred thousand euros in five-hundred-euro notes did not weigh heavily, as they had noticed yesterday.

Luckily, Suzie had noticed when Irene had made an odd reference to spinach in the video.

"I went to get ice cream from the fridge the other day, and there was spinach in the freezer," she recalled. 'Could that be it?'

To their great astonishment, they had found a stack of cash in the package. The notes had been a little damp, but well preserved and quite genuine.

Pep wondered how Irene had come by such amounts of cash. He fervently hoped that Irene would return safely. Then it was time to exchange a few honest words. He would lay his heart at her feet. If ... if only she would listen. The most important thing was that she was healthy and would be set free.

Carlos behind him cleared his throat.

Pep made a sign to follow him. They stopped at the restaurant 'Confraria del Port' and made sure to merge with the shadow. Their eyes were glued to Suzie's figure. The yoga disciple moved loosely and smoothly. Nothing betrayed how nervous she was. She had just moaned, "I can't do it". The two men had talked her through it. The kidnappers had given clear instructions.

Pep, Carlos, Xavi and Suzie had decided to follow them yesterday so as not to endanger Irene even more. Xavi had made a nasty face at the game. He would have preferred to call his father to help and get the Mossos involved. Pep had been able to talk him out of it. Had it been the right thing to do? Professionals might have been able to launch an attack here. But his chest tightened at the thought that the kidnappers might have secured themselves against police intervention and would

make Irene suffer for it. They were no beginners, as the whole procedure showed.

Again, he peeked around the corner. Suzie had almost reached the
small, red lighthouse. There was not a soul in sight far and wide. Maybe
the kidnappers were planning a scavenger hunt? Sending them from
one place to another? His ideas were influenced by films and television,
he had to admit to himself. At that moment he heard a whirring in the
air. He looked up.

CHAPTER SIXTY-FIVE

IRENE HEARD footsteps behind the door. A little dragging, short steps. She recognised the rhythm. The Latino was bringing her food. She had been standing next to the door frame for half an hour now, clutching the table leg. She imagined thundering it on the guy's head, he went down and she stepped over him to freedom.

But now her knees were trembling. What if they came in pairs? But she only heard one person approaching. But what if the other one caught her while she was trying to leave the building? And outside, that huge dog was lurking. A key scratched in the keyhole.

She had to decide quickly. She stepped back from the door, hastily jammed the table leg back into its usual place under the table and scurried over to the bed. At that moment the door opened, the Latino, who was wearing an AC/DC T-shirt today, came in carrying a tray in front of him. It smelled of coffee.

"Buenos días, guapa!"

He had never talked much before, now he sounded in a good mood. Was that a good sign? Irene got her hopes up. She answered with a distant 'Good morning'.

"If all goes well, you'll be home tonight."

Could that be true? Joy sprouted in her.

"We have nothing against you, only Hubert ..."

He pronounced the name like 'Chubert'.

"Hubert set us up, he was punished for it. We need to be able to rely on our transporters."

He put the tray on the table.

"When we have our money, we're even."

Irene held her breath. She didn't want the table leg to give way, which she had just jammed under it in a hurry.

She cleared her throat to make the man turn to her. What on earth could she say to distract him? "Where did Hubert get the money anyway?" Okay, that was the stupidest thing she could think of, she scolded herself.

The man stared at her. "Hubert stole it from us. Thought he was smarter than us."

It was just like him, he had always considered himself more intelligent than others, perhaps only Manfred van Vreeden's sharp mind had been superior to him. But intelligence is not everything in life, Irene told herself. And "Transporter?" So Hubert had actually transported drugs to Germany for the Colombians? She didn't get around to asking.

The Latino said, "Now eat." He nodded to her and left.

The key turned in the lock. Irene heaved a sigh of relief. Fortunately, the table leg had withstood the weight of the breakfast. Next to the plastic cup of coffee was a paper plate with a croissant on the tray. The kidnappers were careful not to give her any porcelain dishes. She could brake those and use the shards as a weapon, she reasoned. But if she didn't even dare knock out a little man with a table leg, she probably wasn't really dangerous.

Was it true what he had said? That she could be home again tonight? With Suzie?

CHAPTER SIXTY-SIX

THE WHIRRING sound in the air came closer. A moving object flew towards Suzie, who looked up in fright.

The object landed at their feet. It had white propellers, and a camera eye.

"A drone," Carlos whispered, sounding awestruck. "Shit, they're smart!"

Pep watched tensely as Suzie took the backpack off her shoulder, pulled out a small packet and fiddled with the drone, attaching the money underneath it. She stood back and the drone took off again. It buzzed towards the harbour, where a fishing boat was just chugging in. A flock of seagulls circled the boat, screeching excitedly.

Suzie came back to them. Pep watched the drone intently. Maybe he could estimate in which direction it was flying. Where the kidnappers were waiting for it. As the fishing boat came closer, the drone crossed its path, flew over the mast at a few metres height. A seagull swooped down on it and pecked at the drone's propellers with its beak.

Pep saw a white part fall off the drone. One of the propeller blades. Then the drone circled around itself and sank downwards. It slapped the surface of the water. A wave washed over it. The drone sank. The fishing boat continued through the waves, reaching the harbour entrance and the calmer waters. The seagulls screeched even louder. They knew that a feast was waiting for them when the fishermen unloaded. Carlos, Pep and Suzie stared at each other in bewilderment.

"Shit," Suzie snapped.

"What now?" asked Carlos. His face was as white as a sheet.

Pep felt a stab through his heart. The ransom delivery had failed. Still worse: the money was gone.

"Can that ..." He cleared his throat, a lump sitting in his throat. "Can a diver bring that back up?"

He pointed to the general area where the drone had gone down. Carlos shrugged his shoulders. Suzie rubbed her nose. All three looked at the dark water of the harbour. The ransom was gone. Irretrievably lost. And none of them could come up with such an amount of cash straight away, he suspected. A pensioner, a yoga teacher and a Gestor in the middle of a divorce case - they couldn't raise hundreds of thousands. At least not overnight.

"There was a Velcro strap on the drone. That's where I attached the package with the money," said Suzie. She ran her hand through her hair. "But will it hold underwater? Can you track the drone, like a mobile phone or something?"

Pep had no idea. He now had to take a step that he had shied away from all this time. This adventure was getting beyond him. Professionals were needed.

He would talk to Xavi later. Maybe he could get the Mossos' machine moving - 'no cops!' or not. Now it was a matter of Irene's life. For surely the hijackers had watched the drone camera transmission and witnessed the crash.

How would they react? What would they do to Irene?

CHAPTER SIXTY-SEVEN

IRENE PACED UP and down the room. In the meantime, she could estimate approximately what time it was from the strip of light between the boards in front of the window. About nine, she would say. If Suzie had found the money in the fridge, if she had come to an agreement with the kidnappers, then she would soon be free. If ... if ... There was nothing left for her to do but hope.

The key in the door turned. It was the usual time for breakfast. The Colombian brought the tray with breakfast. Today he wore the T-shirt with AC/DC written on it again. And, of course, the motorbike mask. In a sense, that was comforting. As long as she couldn't identify anyone, her life was not in danger, she told herself. After all, she had seen enough crime scenes on TV to find this conclusion logical.

"Any reaction to the video yet?"

The question had just slipped out of her mouth.

"Shit happens." The Colombian sounded bitter. "Lost money."

"What, lost money?"

"Money gone!"

He put the tray down on the little table and turned back towards the door.

"Wait a minute! What's happened? What are we going to do?"

Suddenly she felt like she was in the same boat as the kidnappers. If they didn't reach their destination, she wouldn't see freedom again.

"We have to make new video! More pressure!"

The Colombian turned to her once more. She could not make out his face, except for the black eyes peering through the slit in the mask. Still, she was sure he was smiling wickedly. "Jasmin in Hamburg? Shall we videotape her too?"

He turned around and left.

Irene's knees went weak. She slumped down on the bed and began to sob. They knew her and her family very well. Who knows what Hubert had told them? Or if they had spied on him? Jasmin couldn't be dragged into this.

She desperately remembered how the last telephone conversation with Jasmin had ended. In an argument, that is. Over something as stupid as vegan breakfast. Irene swallowed, composed herself and straightened up again, looking around. There had to be a way to get out of here.

CHAPTER SIXTY-EIGHT

"PLAY THE VIDEO AGAIN." Pep could hardly bear to hear Irene's voice and see her desperate face, but somehow they had to carry on. All three stared at the clip stored on Suzie's phone. The lighting conditions were poor; only an overhead lamp seemed to illuminate the room. Irene was sitting on a bed holding this newspaper in front of her. Like ETA kidnappings in the eighties and nineties, Pep thought. On one hand it looked ridiculous, on the other threatening. These guys were using a drone, they certainly weren't dumb.

An image rose up in him that he had seen this morning but had not really noticed. Something he had seen at the harbour. A man wearing sunglasses. No, it hadn't been sunglasses, but something more massive.

He began to explain, what he had seen.

Suzie and Carlos listened to his confused explanation without interrupting him. Carlos cleared his throat. "I don't know that much about technology, but my nephew, he has a drone too. I think with the first person view transmission on digital glasses you can see what the drone sees." He broke off, then added, "The drone does have a camera."

Pep nodded. Yes, the drone must have had a camera. Then the man at the harbour was one of the hijackers. He had watched them and controlled the drone. Witnessed the copter's demise. So the kidnappers knew the ransom money had sunk into the water. That meant, "Irene is in danger. If the kidnappers have no hope of trading their hostage for the money ..." He did not speak any further.

"Oh, my God," was all Suzie said. She understood immediately what he meant.

"We have to get the police involved," Carlos said seriously. "This number is too big for us. I've seen a lot of things in St. Pauli in the past, but this ..."

"I know someone who knows someone."

For better or worse, he had to inform Xavi, Pep told himself. Xavi would then get his father and thus the Mossos on board.

"Play the video again," Suzie said.

Pep held her mobile phone in his hand. Now he clicked the arrow for 'Play' again.

"And turn the sound up!"

He followed the instruction. Suzie closed her eyes and listened. Pep already knew the words by heart. He hated hearing Irene so stressed.

"Pull over."

He pressed the pause button.

"There's a noise in the background, isn't there? A bark?"

He rewound the video and ran it again. Suzie was right. A dark, angry bark could be heard.

"So what? Dogs are yapping all over the place," he said.

"It's certainly not a handbag dog. Not one of those lap animals you carry around as a mascot."

"That sounds more like a guard dog." Carlos agreed with her.

"Wait a minute, Irene told me something about a Doberman she saw in a hotel complex in Salou ..."

"She what ...?" Pep was horrified.

Suzie told them what Irene had reported to her.

"She was snooping around there by herself?"

Pep felt a cold hand reach for his heart. He thought of the stories of the Colombian mafia that Xavi had told him. If the kidnapping involved such dimensions, there were no amateurs involved.

"I told her it was far too dangerous," Suzie said lamely.

Pep pulled out his mobile phone, dialled Xavi.

"Xavi? We need your help!"

He listened for a while. He didn't like what Xavi told him at all. Then he thanked him and ended the conversation.

"The police are not an option."

"Why?" asked Suzie.

"Why not?" came from Carlos at the same time.

"The latest actions against the Colombians have been leaked. The dates of house searches have been given away. It seems someone in the police is on the Kapos' payroll."

"Then we'll have to do it ourselves," Carlos said resolutely.

"We must not endanger Irene," warned Suzie, who had turned pale.

"A police operation gone wrong is worse than none at all. Especially after the fiasco with the drone. But Xavi has another suggestion."

The two looked at him tensely.

"The colla will help us."

CHAPTER SIXTY-NINE

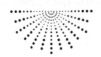

PEP FOLLOWED Xavi and the others out of the colla. He tried to get his bearings. The lights from the town did not shine up the hill to here. The grounds of the new hotel complex were vast and in complete darkness. There were no streetlights or other lamps here.

He neither heard nor saw them, but hoped that Suzie and Carlos were approaching from the street as agreed. They had changed into their tight-fitting, garishly coloured yoga clothes. If they encountered anyone, they would claim she was looking for a quiet place for night yoga. They would look like naive tourists and provide a distraction while Pep and the colla invaded the compound from behind.

There was only one problem. They were standing in front of a massive wall two metres high. While Pep was still looking up at the perimeter, Xavi pushed him aside. He used hand signals to direct some burly men and two petite women forward. When the pap de colla had informed his people about the upcoming action, the women had insisted on going along.

Now a pillar formed in the blink of an eye. The women climbed nimbly up the men and reached the crown of the wall in no time. It seemed effortless. One by one, they pulled the other members of the group up. Pep felt like a wet sack. Unlike the castellers, it was difficult for him to overcome the obstacle despite the support. But from below the men pushed, from above hands reached out to him. With a groan, he too made it over the wall. On the other side he jumped down and was caught by helping arms so that his impact was cushioned.

After a few minutes, everyone had reached the grounds of the hotel complex. The well-rehearsed castellers team had shown its strength. They crept across a withered lawn towards the huts, whose locations could only be guessed at in the darkness. At that moment, Pep stepped on a dry branch that broke under his feet. The sound echoed through the night. Pep stood transfixed and held his breath. Then Xavi pushed him further forward.

Now they crept down the trail to approach the hotel grounds from behind. The huts were scattered on the slope, their whitewashed walls standing out against the dark background. Was Irene really here? And if so, in which building? They had no choice but to search one after the other.

Then he sensed movement at one of the huts. He tapped Xavi on the shoulder and silently pointed in that direction. They crept toward the hut. A point of light came on. At the same moment, Pep smelled cigarette smoke. He grabbed Xavi by the sleeve. He tapped him on the upper arm to confirm that he had also noticed the smoker, as Pep had hoped. Then everything happened very quickly. Pep ran and threw himself at the smoker. He let out a yelp, but Pep had already put his hand over his mouth.

A clicking sound. Xavi had ignited the lighter and was holding it to the man's face, who blinked in irritation. A Latino. He was wearing a black shirt with AC/DC written on it in white. Bad taste in music, Pep thought, and at the same time was irritated that he even gave it a thought.

Xavi pulled a green plastic string out of his pocket. It looked like a piece of clothesline. He tied the Latino's hands and feet.

"If you scream, you're dead," Pep threatened him, although he knew full well that he would never be able to kill the guy. He was no ninja warrior. If all went well, they would hand the kidnappers over to the Mossos. Pep hoped they would take over when they were presented with the perpetrators on a platter, if only to take credit,. Even if some of the Mossos were on the payroll of the Colombian capos.

"Where's Irene?", he demanded.

The Latino made a head movement in the direction of the hut.

So we are on the right track.

Pep searched the man's trouser pockets. A key! He took it. Then he pulled the guy's T-shirt half over his head and knotted it at the back of his head. The Latino could no longer see anything and you couldn't hear him shout through the fabric.

They left him behind.

The door was ajar. The man had only come out for a quick smoke, so he had saved himself the trouble of locking it. Pep pushed his way through the door. Xavi pressed close to him, always staying in close contact, and followed. The men and women of the Colla stayed close behind them. A small hallway, a chair.

They stopped and listened. Nothing to hear. Yet Pep sensed the presence of another person. An empty building simply felt different from an inhabited one. Someone was near here, he felt it like a vibration in the air. Carlos nudged him from behind. Slowly, Pep put one foot in front of the other, crept down the hall to the door. He put the key they had taken from the Latino into the lock.

Turned it.

Opened the door and stepped into a dark room.

He felt a draft.

Something banged on his skull.

His eyes went black.

CHAPTER SEVENTY

SHE HAD STRUCK with all her might. The table leg had hit the skull with a hollow crack. But this was not the Latino who had always brought her food. At her feet lay a tall man with flaxen hair - his sea-blue eyes rolled back.

Another big guy came in the door, pulled her roughly into his arms. "My dear" He squeezed her with a bear hug. Carlos! She wriggled out of his grasp and slumped to her knees. "Pep!" She put her hand to his neck and felt around.

The skin was warm. She felt something under her fingers. The pulse! "He's alive!"

Carlos lowered himself lithely to the floor. He opened Pep's jacket. Rolled the man onto his side and pulled his knees in. Then he had already pulled out his mobile phone. "We need an ambulancia!" In broken Spanish, he announced where they were.

"What have I done!" Irene sobbed out. She threw herself against Carlos' chest again. A flood of tears shot from her eyes.

"Easy, my dear." He patted her back reassuringly.

A group of men came into the room. Irene flinched, but it was not the kidnappers, but Xavi and his team from the Castellers. Well-trained women and men with determined expressions on their faces. But they were too late. Then a hand reached for Irene's.

"Suzie!" Irene broke away from Carlos and fell around Suzie's neck in return.

"What have you been through, dear?" Suzie's voice sounded worried.

Irene regained her composure. She loosened her embrace and took a step back. Pep was lying on his side and breathing, albeit weakly.

"I messed up the money transfer," Suzie blurted out. "Sorry, I'm so sorry. Otherwise you would have been free last night."

One night more or less doesn't matter anymore, Irene thought. At the same moment she knew that this was not true. Every single hour she had spent here weighed heavily. She never wanted to be locked up again, she knew that now.

She answered something completely different: "And this one I messed up." She pointed at Pep.

The man still looked attractive even in his unconsciousness. She had rejected him when they had run into each other while cleaning up after the storm. And now he had apparently moved heaven and hell to help her. She bit her lower lip. Then she went down on her knees and took his hand in hers. It felt cold.

CHAPTER SEVENTY-ONE

A JACKHAMMER WORKED NEXT to his ear. Pep blinked. The jackhammer was not working next to his ear, but directly on the top of his skull. Was he in a construction site? Panic gripped his heart. He wrenched his eyes open.

The dominant white blinded him, he squinted his eyes again. Next to the jackhammer, a whirring jigsaw set to work. Not a building site, perhaps an operation without anaesthetic? Had he woken up in the middle of it?

Pep grunted.

Someone reached for his hand. "Pep? Are you awake?"

A woman started sobbing.

I guess it wasn't surgery after all. Or was the attending crying because she just lost her patient?

He didn't feel that bad after all.

Pep opened his eyes again, slowly.

Someone stroked his hand.

He tried to turn his head to see who was sitting next to him, but immediately felt sick. He paused in his movement.

"Shh, don't move!" The stroking continued. It calmed him. "You're in the hospital. I was so scared for you."

He knew the voice. It belonged to someone he liked. Very much. He remembered that. But who was it?

Darkness descended upon him.

When he woke up again, the jackhammer was a hammer. He could still feel it, but it no longer seemed to be directly against his skull.

Again someone reached for his hand and squeezed it.

"I'm so sorry. I thought one of the kidnappers was coming in, so I hit it as hard as I could. I recognised you too late."

The kidnapping! The hotel! Irene! Little by little, some details of the last few days came to him. How had he got into the hotel? He remembered sneaking through the grounds with Carlos. But then? What had happened?

He felt a glass at his lips. He realised that he was tremendously thirsty. His throat was completely parched. Clumsily he took a sip, the glass disappeared.

"More," he brought out.

Again the cool glass at his lips, the refreshing wetness. He drank a few sips, then his head sank back onto the pillow. Accompanied by a firework of pain.

The door rattled. It sounded as if something was being pulled over his skull again.

A bright female voice asked, "Is he awake?"

"Yes, just woke up." Irene whispered considerately, in contrast to the trumpeting nurse.

Again someone took his hand, this time with a firm, professional grip. "The vital signs look good. Obviously a real bear skull. I'll up the pain meds, with this head trauma."

Perhaps the woman chattered on, but his brain dissolved into cotton wool, he slipped back into the blackness that caught him graciously.

CHAPTER SEVENTY-TWO

IRENE IDENTIFIED herself at the entrance to the police headquarters. She held her wet umbrella a little away from her so as not to soak her trouser legs. At the airport, she had been greeted the day before yesterday with drizzle that had not let up.

The security company employee gave her back her ID card and explained how she would find the room.

"Thank you, I know my way around." Kroeger

He greeted her in his quiet way, offered her a chair and coffee, which she gratefully accepted.

"I heard what happened to you. I'm glad you're back safe and sound," he said. Then he pointed in the direction of his computer screen. "Our colleagues from Catalonia have informed us about their investigation, even though the report is still preliminary."

He asked Irene to describe the events from her point of view. She managed to do that without erupting into a crying fit. Again and again, she told herself that it could have been worse. The most important thing was that she was healthy and that Pep had not suffered any serious damage either. The doctors had given the okay for him to go home again as long as he didn't do any strenuous activities. Without this knowledge, she would certainly not have flown to Hamburg.

"Unfortunately, we have not yet been able to identify the perpetrators who killed your husband. The arrest of the Colombians in Spain will help us - if they make a statement."

Volker Kroeger looked at her from sad eyes, as if it was hopeless to expect one. Irene wished she could close the whole story. What good was it to her if the perpetrators disappeared behind bars. That would not bring Hubert back. However, she wanted to know what had led to her husband owing money to the Colombian mafia in the first place. The inspector wondered the same thing.

"Our investigations so far have shown that Hubert Hansen brought cocaine to Hamburg by car as a courier. And regularly, as our contacts from the scene assured us. He certainly belonged to the profile of business travellers who never attracted attention during random customs checks at the border."

Irene nodded.

"The Spanish report that there were irregularities in the construction of the hotel in Salou. Illicit funds are said to have been paid. Hubert Hansen had apparently diverted some money here. We don't know where these funds went."

But Irene knew. The stack of notes was lying on the bottom of the marina in Cambrils. Maybe a diver would be happy about it one day, if sea creatures didn't eat away at the paper money.

"The Colombians are thick in the real estate business on the coast down there," Kroeger continued. "They knew exactly what Hubert Hansen had been shooting. That's why they were able to put pressure on him and force him to smuggle the drugs to Germany. Not an uncommon procedure - there are hundreds of such couriers who bring small quantities into the country. This is much more inconspicuous than the spectacular deliveries in overseas containers, which blow up every now and then. But even there, a lot goes through without the customs colleagues noticing." He looked up: "You guessed it, understaffing, overwork, insufficient equipment - I don't want to complain too loudly about how we are treated."

Irene nodded. She did not want to get into a discussion, but already the cheap furniture in Kroeger's office showed that equipping the Criminal Investigation Unit did not seem to be one of the municipality's most urgent tasks.

"I can't tell you any more than that at the moment. When we have completed the investigation, you will be informed. But your husband's accounts have now been released."

"What about those wallets? The accounts for Bitcoins?"

"Oh yes, there was something else." He glanced over his reading glasses. His eyes were alert and intelligent. "The words you transmitted to us were indeed the seed phrases."

Irene had found a book of poems in Hubert's bedside table in Hamburg, which had surprised her, because he rarely read, and when he did, it was crime novels. Inside the poetry book was a note with English words like 'moon', 'sister', 'bridge', 'alright'. Words that made no sense. But they reminded her of Kroeger's demand.

"We were able to access the wallets, but they are empty. We can track the transactions via the blockchain. They end up at an online exchange where the crypto assets were exchanged for euros and dollars and paid out on a credit card."

"A credit card?"

"Yes, it belonged to a certain Manfred van Vreeden. However, he cannot be found at his home address."

Irene swallowed. "My husband's colleague."

"We assume that the two were in cahoots. Otherwise he would not have had access to the wallets."

That made sense. She thought of how van Vreeden had tried to stop her from looking through the files in Hubert's office. How he had suddenly turned up in Catalonia to stick his nose into the matter of the hotel complex. She told Kroeger about it and added: "Maybe he wanted to check whether the dirty money deals with the hotel could still blow up. Whether there were any loose threads."

"I think so too. The public prosecutor's office has put out an international APB on him."

She had to sign a protocol, then she said goodbye to Kroeger, who wished her well.

As she walked through the Hamburg rain back to the hotel, the city's first climate-friendly hotel, she thought of Madlen, who was probably now strutting across the Copacabana on Van Vreeden's arm. Or wallowing with him on a Caribbean beach. The thought no longer hurt. The girl had looked for a new sugar daddy and had fallen for the wrong one again. Van Vreeden was involved in the affair with the hotel in Salou. Sooner or later Interpol would find him. The renowned architectural firm VHB was history. She was not the least bit sorry.

EPILOGUE

ONE MONTH LATER ...

SMALL WAVES WASHED around Irene's feet. She sported a pink nail varnish on her toes that she had discovered in one of the boutiques on the beach promenade. She liked the way the water played around her toes, retreating again. A fringe of bubbles remained. Then the next wave arrived.

She gripped Pep tighter and pulled him a little way up the beach, into the area of dry sand. Only then did she feel how ice-cold her feet had become. She noticed something red among all the flotsam and seaweed and bent down curiously. A small rubber ball.

"Hey, Fosca!"

She threw the ball as far as she could.

The dog shot after it. He ran so fast that sand swirled up behind him and his shaggy ears fluttered in the wind.

Pep rushed after Fosca, pretending to take the ball back from her. Irene also ran. When she caught up with Pep, he intercepted her with his arms outstretched, hugged her and kissed her.

What a kiss! Pep's lips were full and strong. His tongue probed out. Without hesitation, Irene opened her mouth. After the kiss, she felt drained.

Pep reached into the pocket of his weather jacket and pulled out a package, which he handed to Irene. "Here, for you!"

Excited, she tore open the paper. "Oh, this is beautiful!" A silk scarf with an organic pattern in pink and grey with black accents unfolded. She held it in front of her with both arms and let it flutter in the wind.

The colours seemed to vibrate.

She remembered the day she had met Pep on the beach and Hubert's Hermès scarf had irrevocably disappeared into the sea. Now she had a replacement. She folded the scarf into a triangle and put it around her neck.

Pep adjusted it a little and closed it with an elegant knot.

"Thank you! Mil gracias!"

She kissed him.

A seagull sailed by and let out a harsh cry.

Pep wrapped Irene in his arms and did not let go. "I hope you'll stay a few more days ... or weeks."

She nodded, lost in thought. The bank had approved the loan for the renovation of the hotel, especially since they were able to contribute a large share of the money from Hubert's accounts. Jasmin was completely absorbed in the choice of organic building materials. Irene was happy not to have to supervise craftsmen. Or even having to find vegan ingredients for a climate-friendly breakfast. Let Jasmin worry about implementing her vision. For now, they had found a compromise: They would continue to serve the traditional breakfast, plus vegan alternatives of their choice. The risk of alienating the regulars was thus averted.

Pep whispered in her ear, "I need you close to me."

She hugged him tighter. Hamburg could wait. If Pep and she continued to get along so well, who knows, maybe she would gradually spend more time with him in Catalonia? Take a bigger flat and sell the flat they lived in together more poorly than well? At the moment it served as a love nest - for Pep and her.

The END

ACKNOWLEDGMENTS

Dear reader,

if you liked the book, I would be happy to receive a rating or review online. As an independent author a little support from readers helps a lot, thank you.

How did this novel come about? When a dangerous virus spread around the world, we didn't yet know about the new disease, kept our distance from other people, and limited our travel. I spent a lot of time at home and longed for faraway places, especially the Mediterranean. As a writer, I used my imagination and beamed myself to beautiful beaches every day. Here you can read the result.

A book is always a work that is created together with many other people. I thank all those who support me.

Simone Wernet commented on the synopsis and thus helped to make the plot flow logically.

Thanks to my dear friend Jordi for corrections of the Catalan expressions.

Thanks to my Facebook friends Claudia Weber-Gebert, Marcel Marcel and Wolfgang Dorsch for information about drones, especially flying with goggles (FPV, First Person View), which the fictional hijackers use here. Wolfgang was the only one of them determined enough to ask what I would use the information for, especially when I asked how to attach the ransom to the copter. Only a look at my website convinced him that it was research for a novel. Thanks to the Castellers from the Colla Xiquets de Cambrils whose training I was allowed to attend. It was exciting to see how they practice for the human towers. I found the informal community in the Colla across all ages and social boundaries impressive.

Thanks to VG Wort for the "Neustart Kultur" grant, which gave me the freedom to focus on my manuscript.

The test readers Maren and Ulrike gave me initial feedback that helped me improve the text.

The English version was translated by DeepL (artificial intelligence).

Last, but not least, I would like to thank PJ Skinner for editing and Amanda Konigs for helping to improve the English translation.

You find my German books under www.katja-kleiber.de.

Yours,

Katja

Milton Keynes UK
Ingram Content Group UK Ltd.
UKHW011112201123
432908UK00007B/1108